SUPERTATO
MEAN GREEN TIME MACHINE

Meet Sue and Paul:

Sue Hendra and **Paul Linnet** have been making books together since 2009 when they came up with *Barry the Fish with Fingers*, and since then they haven't stopped. If you've ever wondered which one does the writing and which does the illustrating, wonder no more . . . they both do both!

For Barney Marriott

FSC
www.fsc.org

MIX
Paper | Supporting
responsible forestry
FSC® C023419

SIMON & SCHUSTER

First published in Great Britain in 2023 by Simon & Schuster UK Ltd • 1st Floor, 222 Gray's Inn Road, London, WC1X 8HB
Text and illustrations copyright © 2023 Sue Hendra and Paul Linnet
The right of Sue Hendra and Paul Linnet to be identified as the authors and illustrators of this work
has been asserted by them in accordance with the Copyright, Designs and Patents Act, 1988
All rights reserved, including the right of reproduction in whole or in part in any form
A CIP catalogue record for this book is available from the British Library upon request
978-1-3985-1167-5 (PB) • 978-1-3985-1168-2 (eBook) • 978-1-3985-1237-5 (eAudio) • Printed in Italy • 10 9 8 7 6 5 4 3 2 1

SUPERTATO
MEAN GREEN TIME MACHINE

SUE HENDRA
PAUL LINNET

SIMON & SCHUSTER
London   New York   Sydney   Toronto   New Delhi

It was night-time in
the supermarket . . .

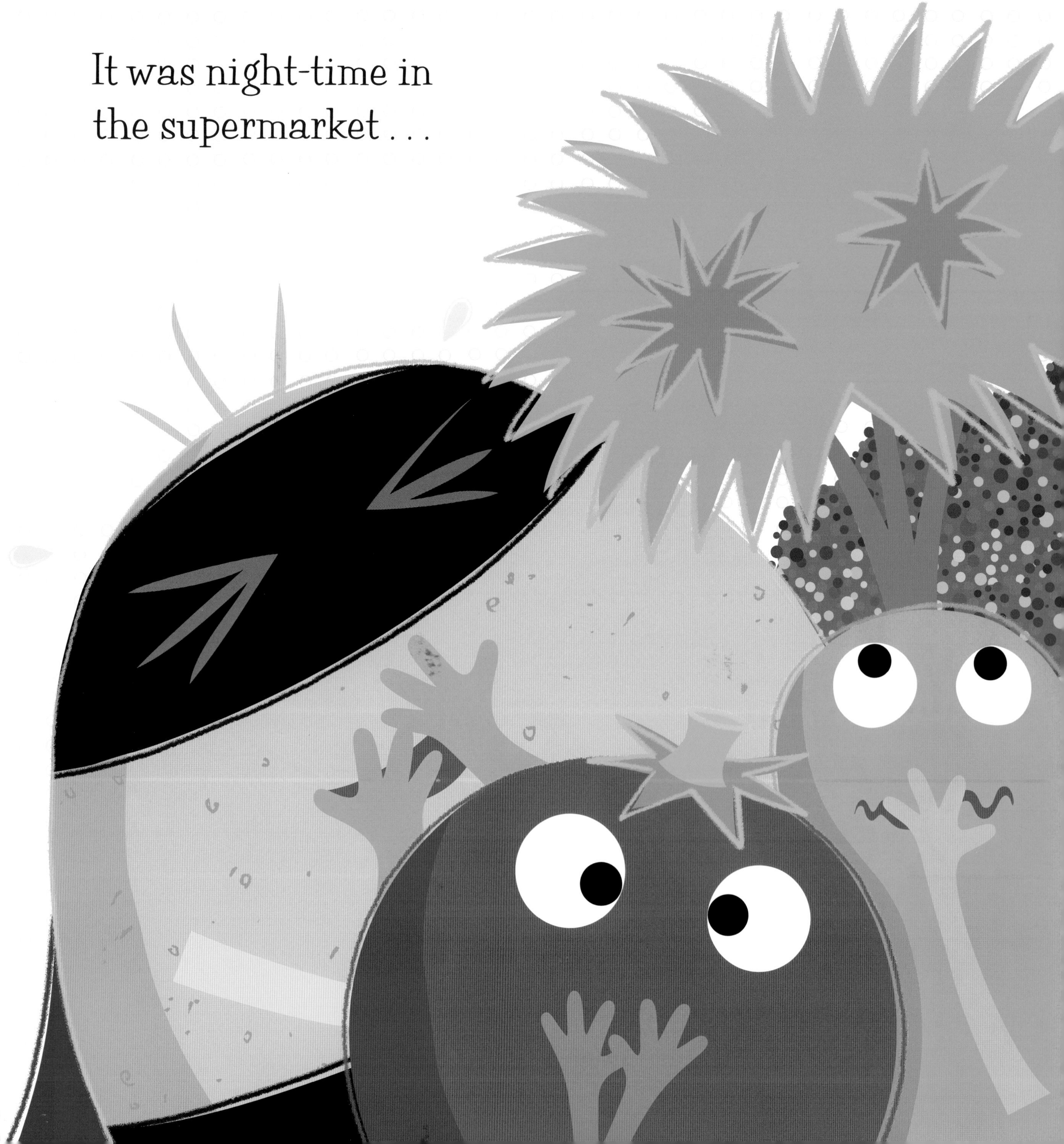

. . . and Supertato and the veggies were trying DESPERATELY . . .

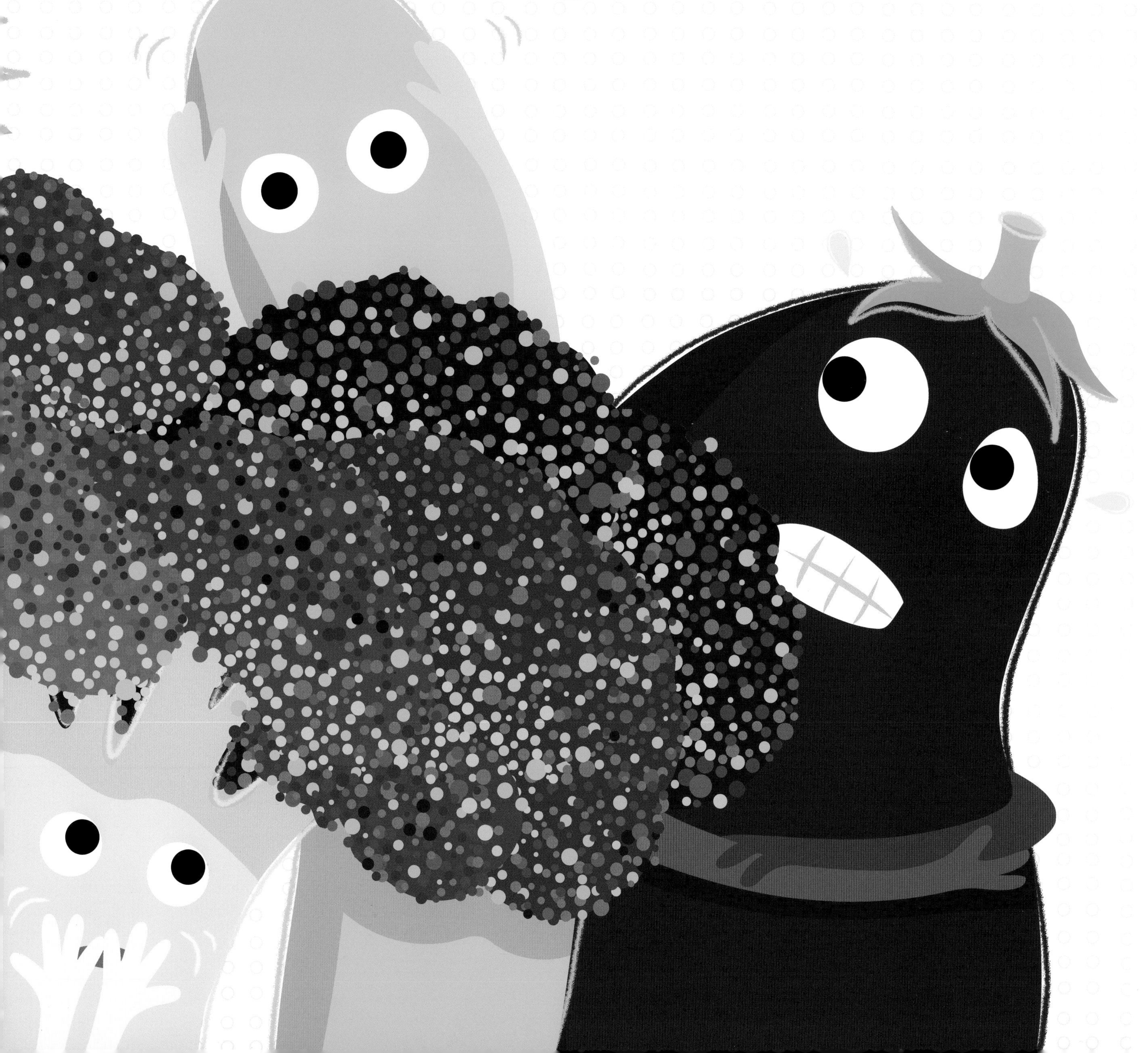

. . . not to laugh at Supertato's baby pictures!

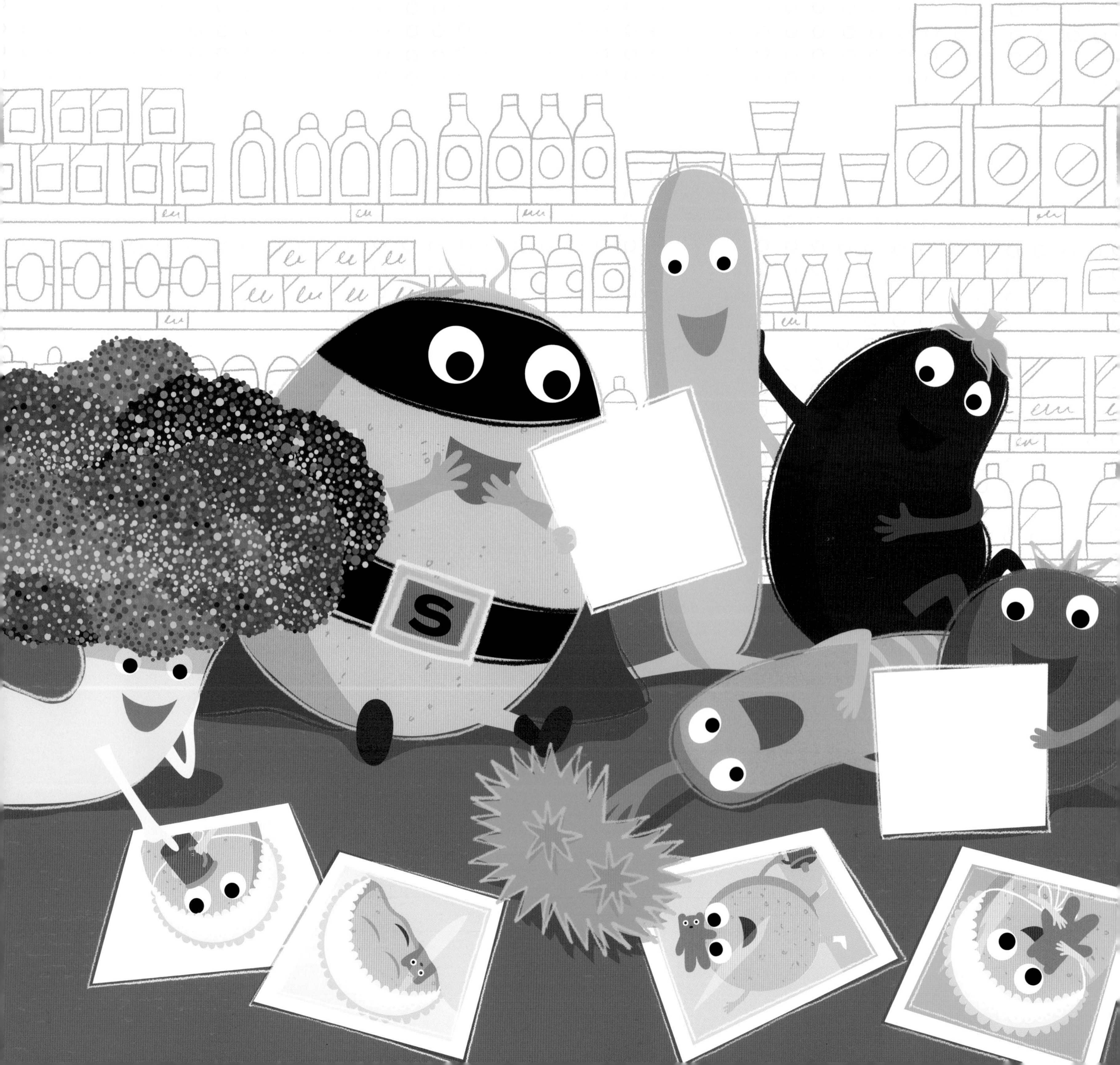
S

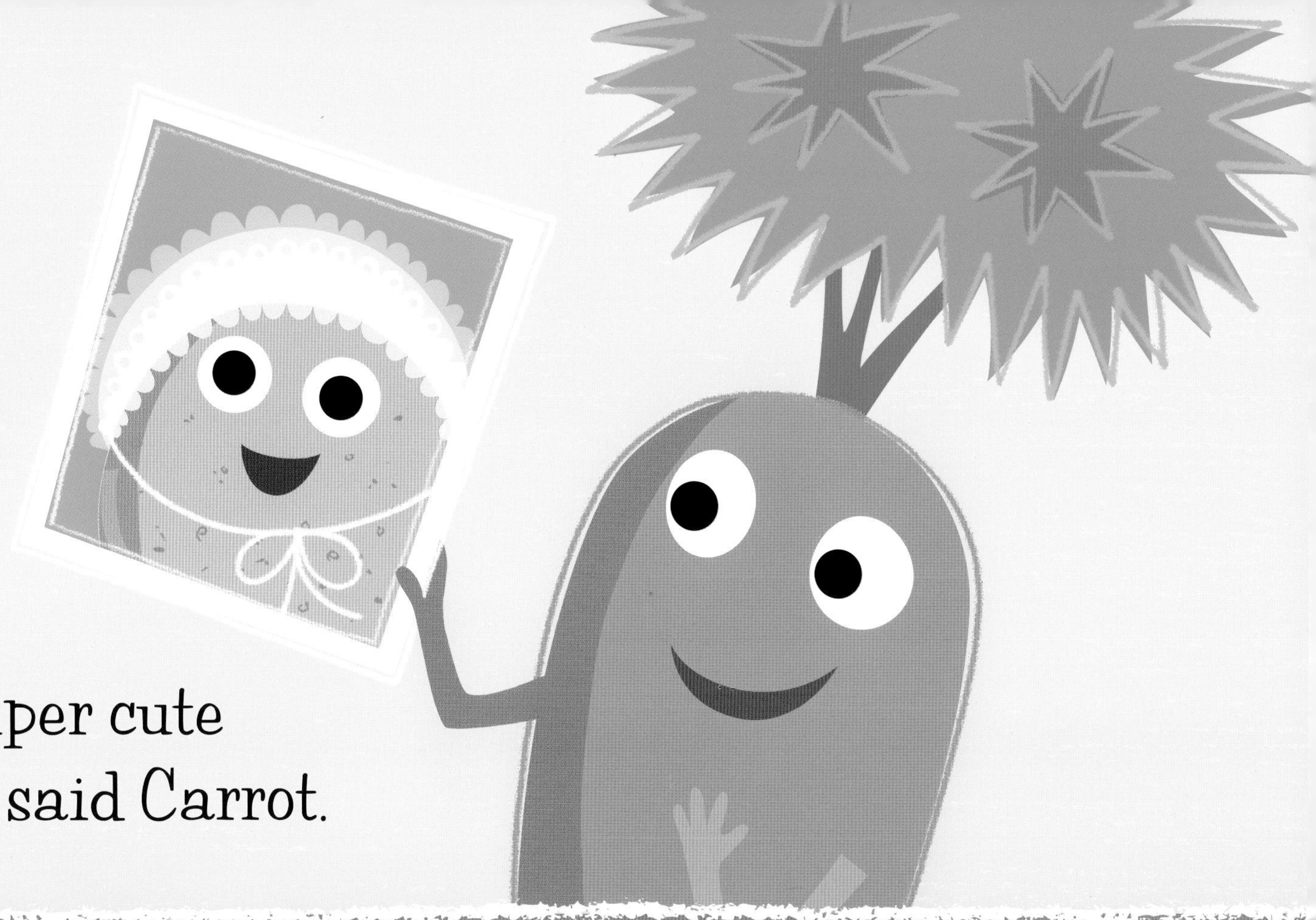

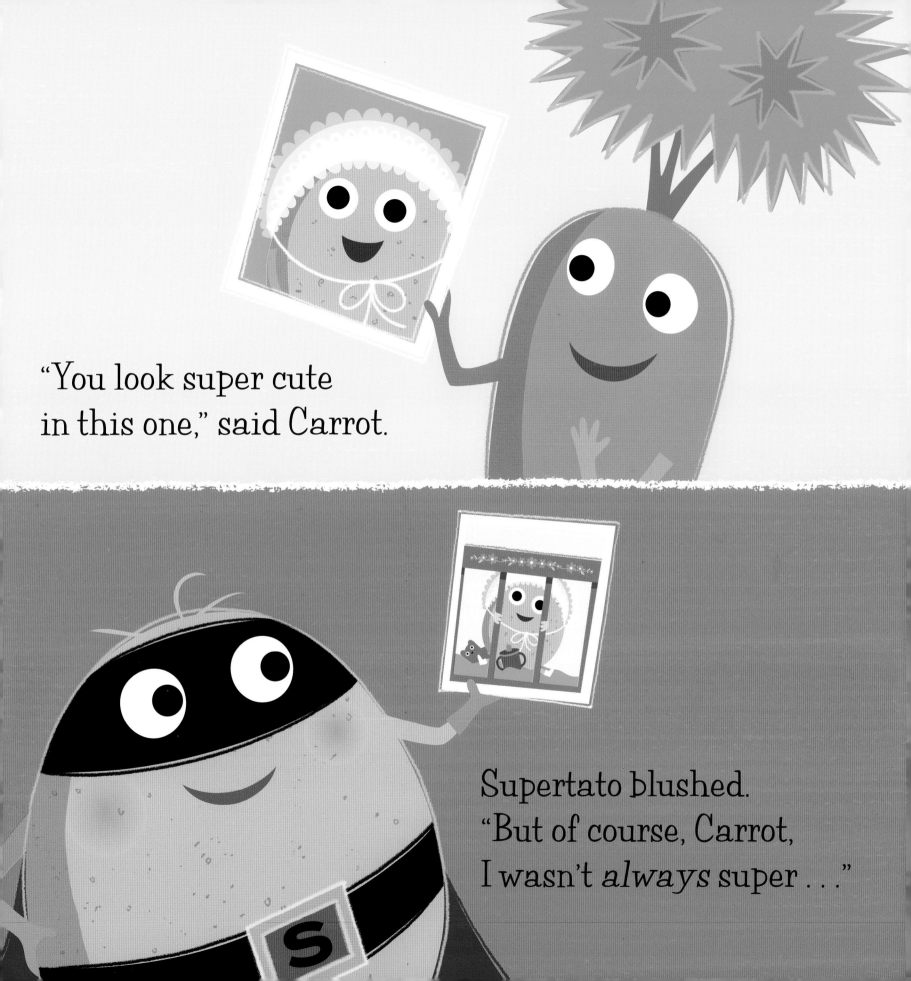

"You look super cute
in this one," said Carrot.

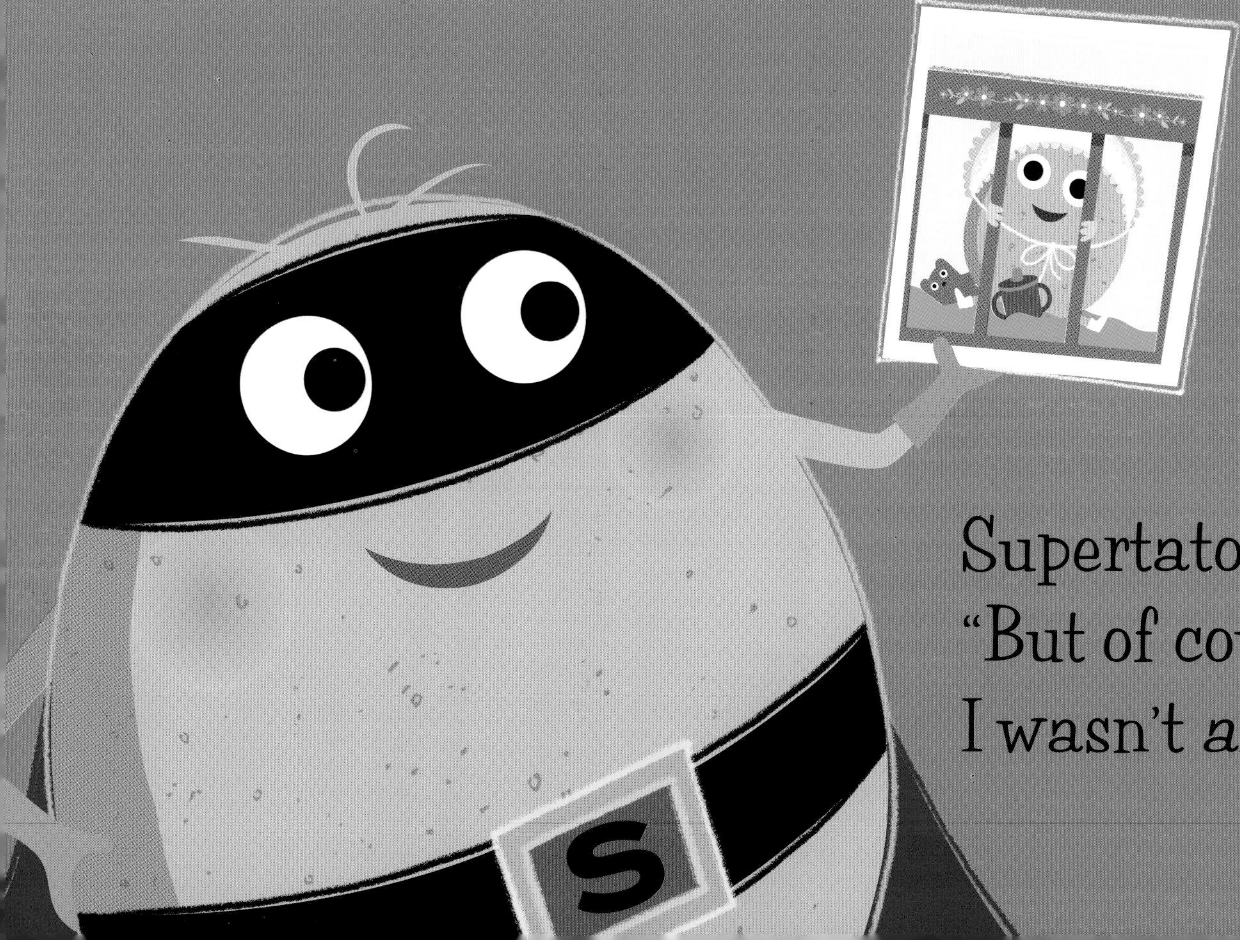
S

Supertato blushed.
"But of course, Carrot,
I wasn't *always* super . . ."

The Evil Pea was listening in.

"Not always SUPER, eh?!
Hmmm, if only I could have got rid of
Supertato **BEFORE** he had any powers . . ."

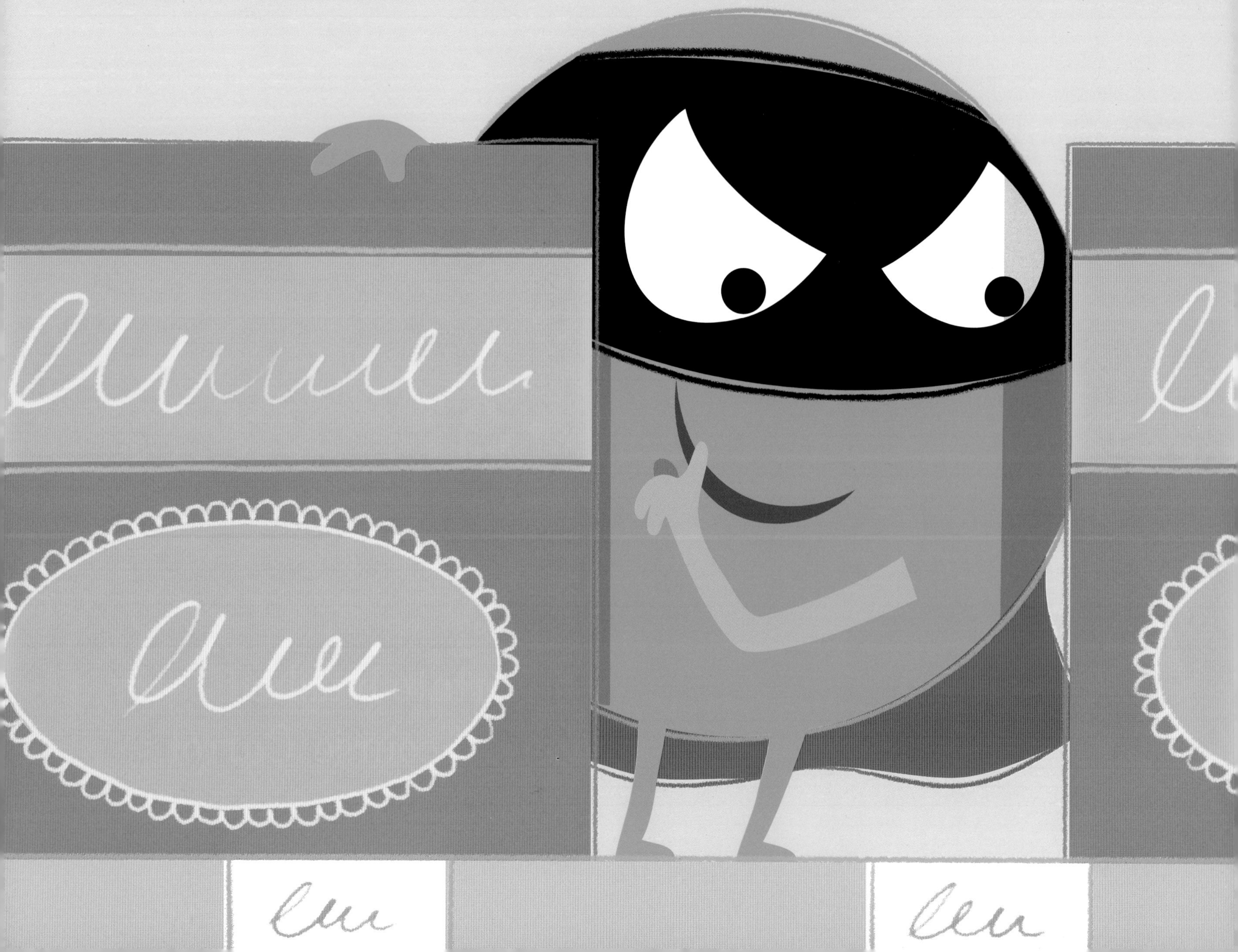

"HA! If only he had a Time Machine," joked one pineapple to another.

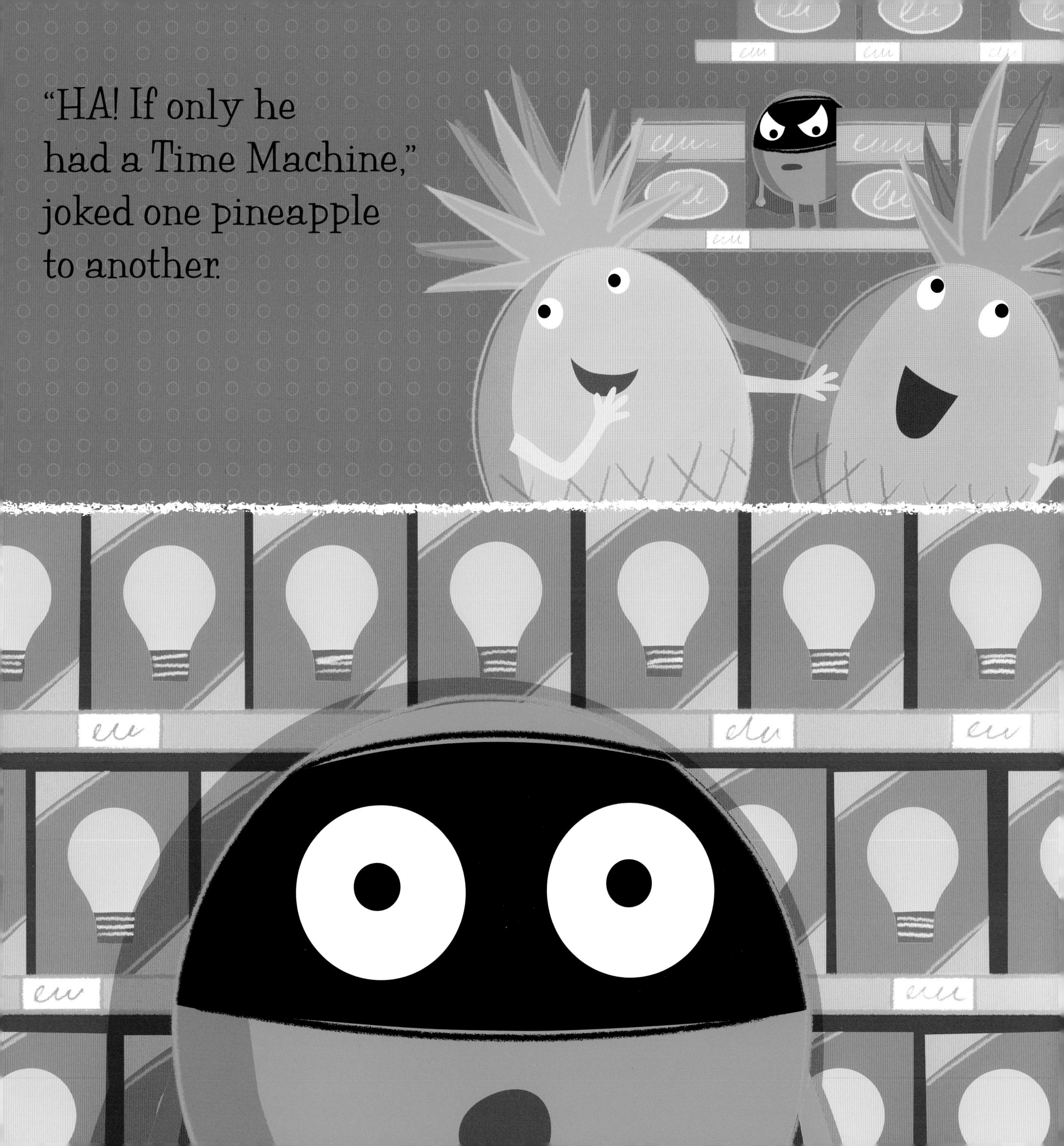

The Evil Pea immediately set to work and it wasn't long before his Time Machine started to take shape.

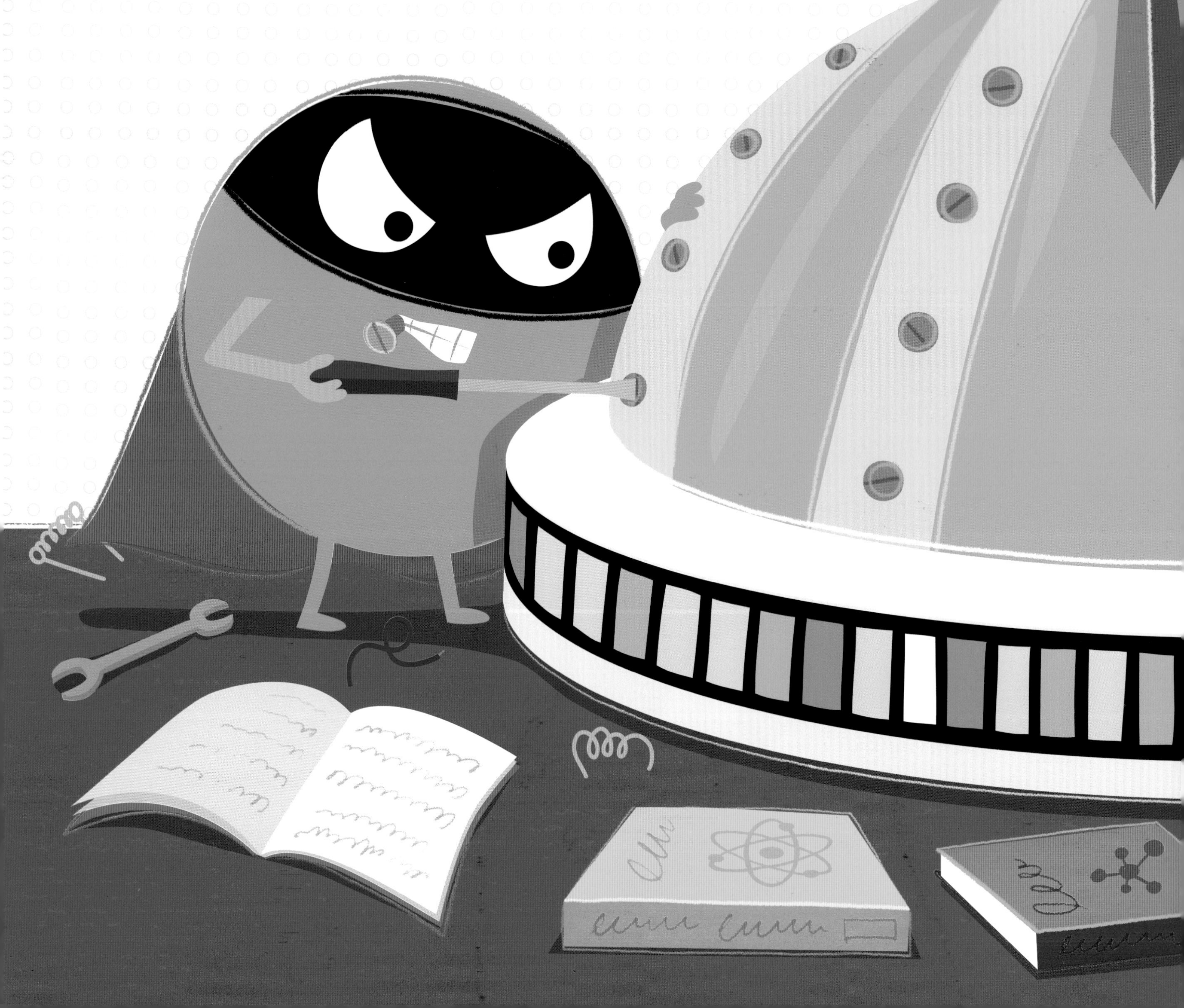

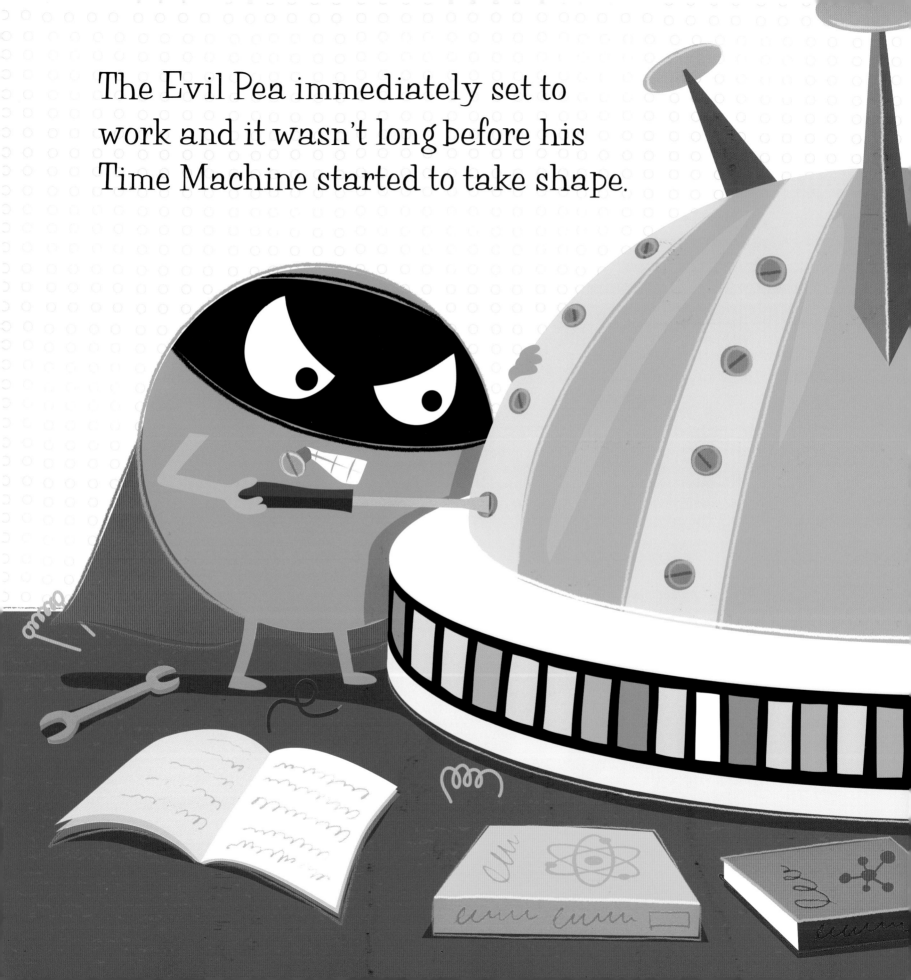

"Now for the tricky bit," muttered the pea. "Making the Time Crystals.

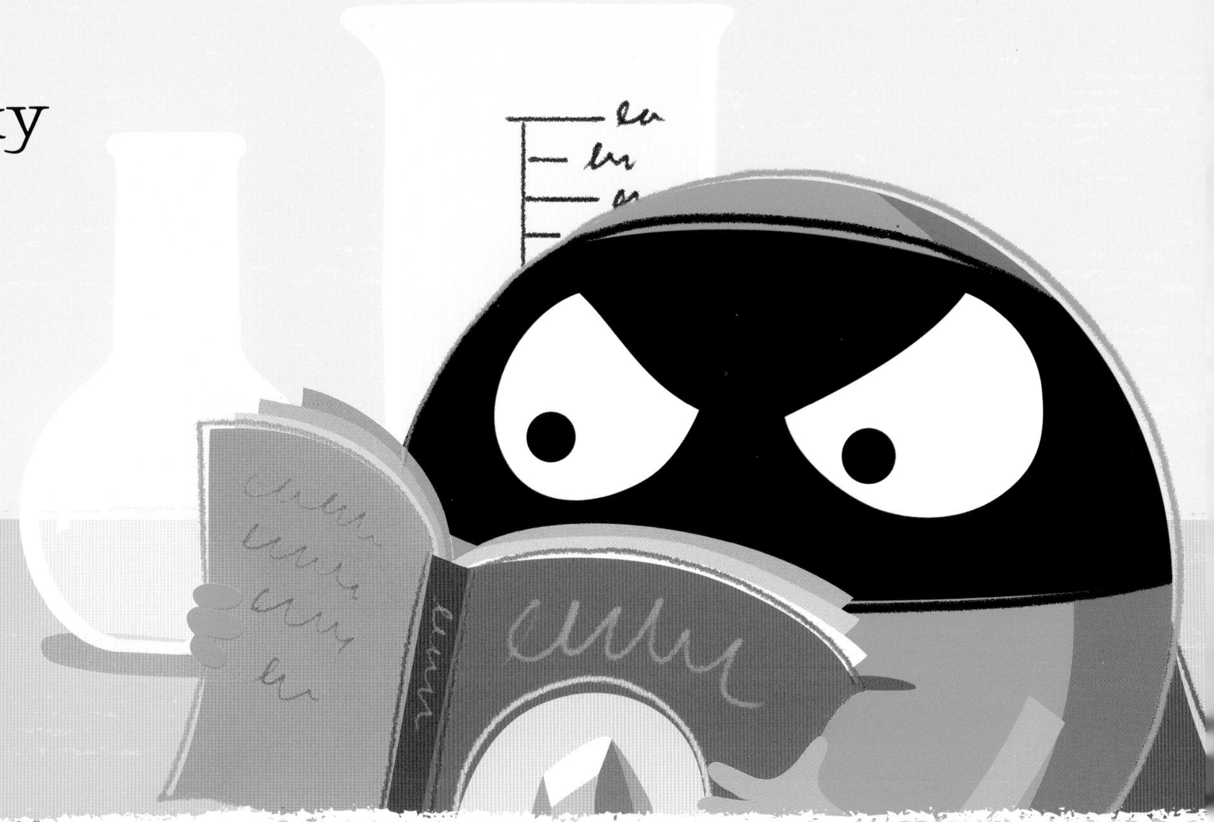

But this recipe can't be right . . ."

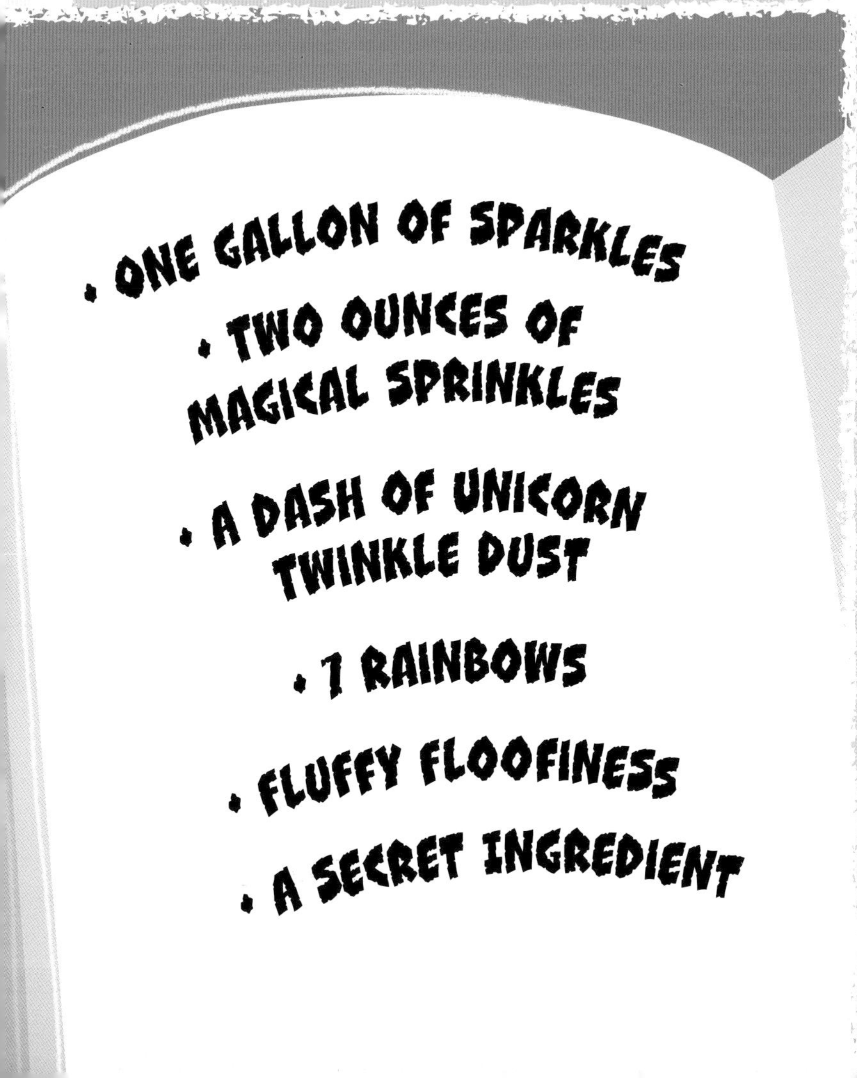
• ONE GALLON OF SPARKLES
• TWO OUNCES OF MAGICAL SPRINKLES
• A DASH OF UNICORN TWINKLE DUST
• 7 RAINBOWS
• FLUFFY FLOOFINESS
• A SECRET INGREDIENT

"Sparkles?!
Magical WHAT??"
spat the pea. But luckily . . .

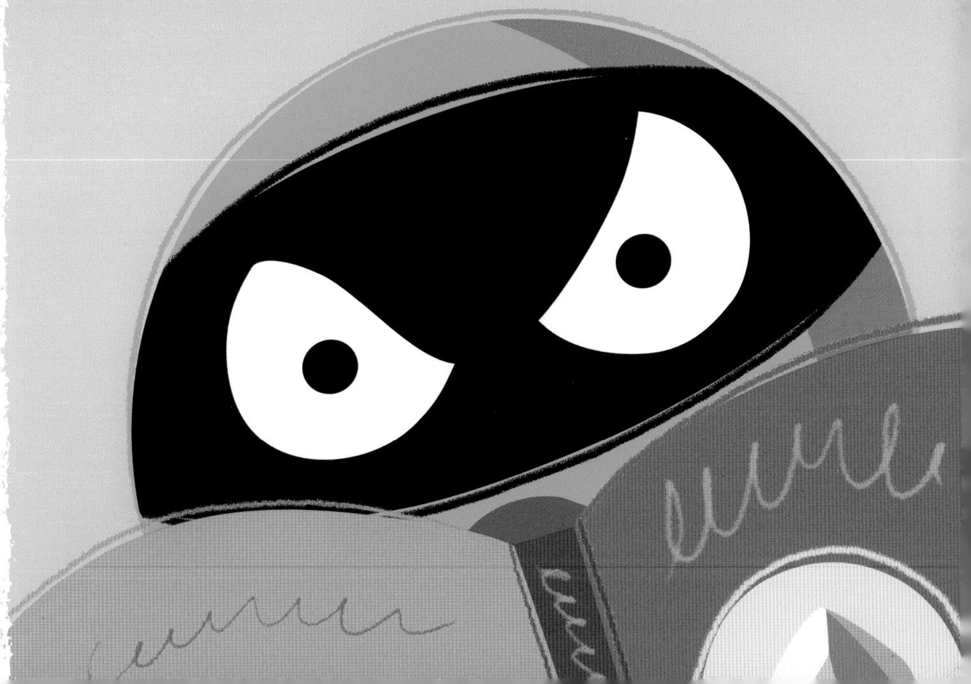

. . . it's surprising
what you can find
in the supermarket . . .

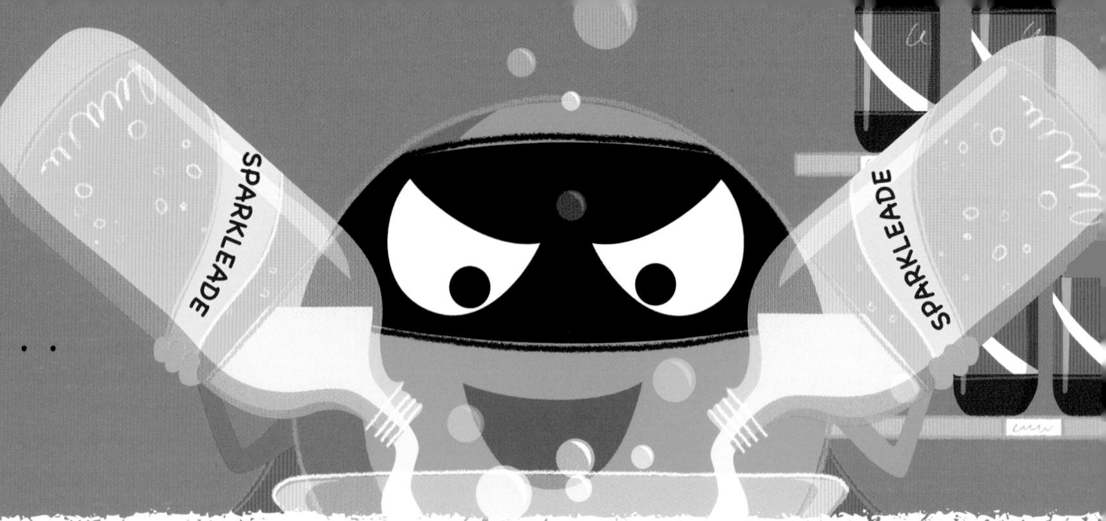
SPARKLEADE
SPARKLEADE

"Ha!

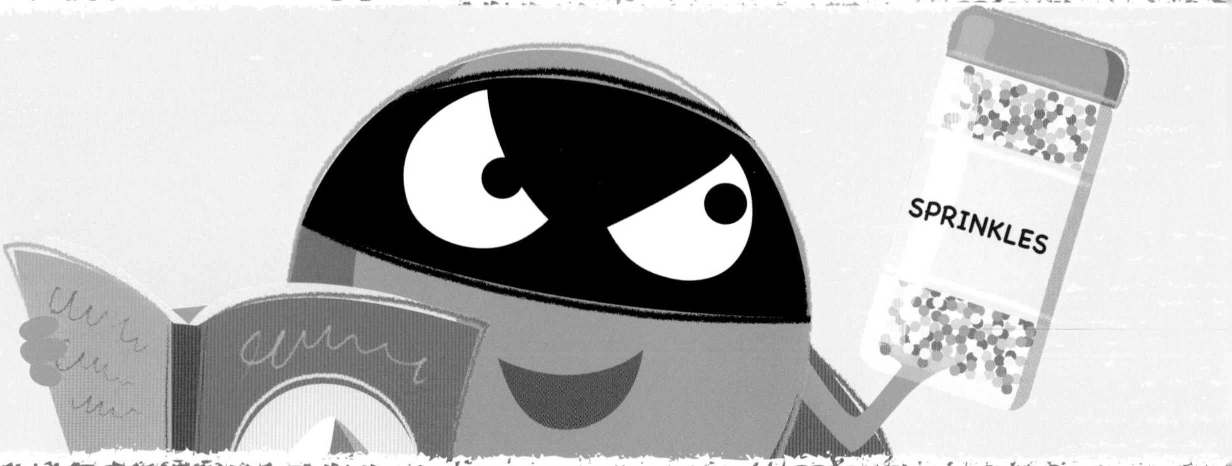
SPRINKLES

Grrrrrrrr!"

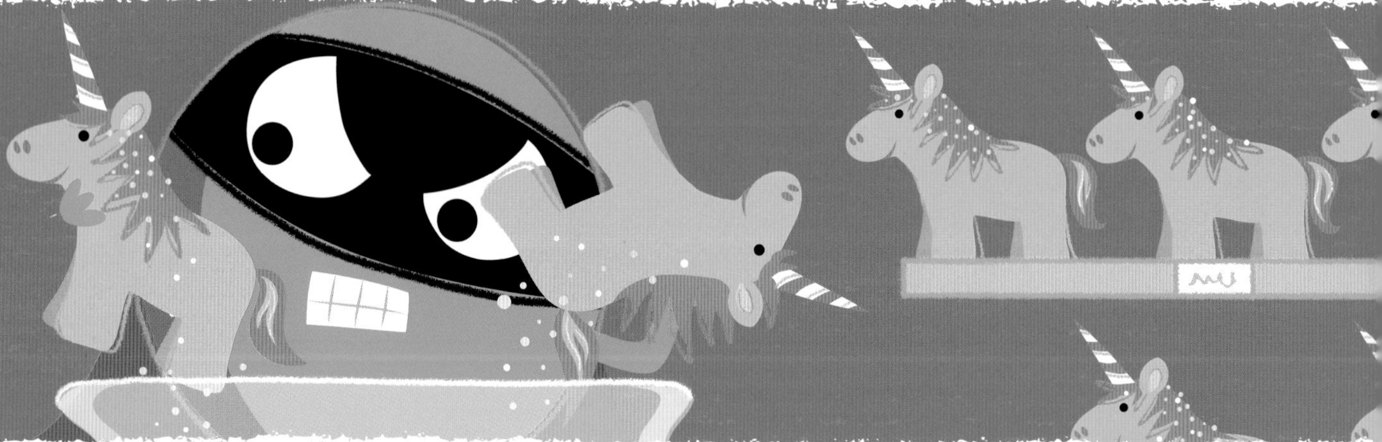

It was all going
rather well until . . .

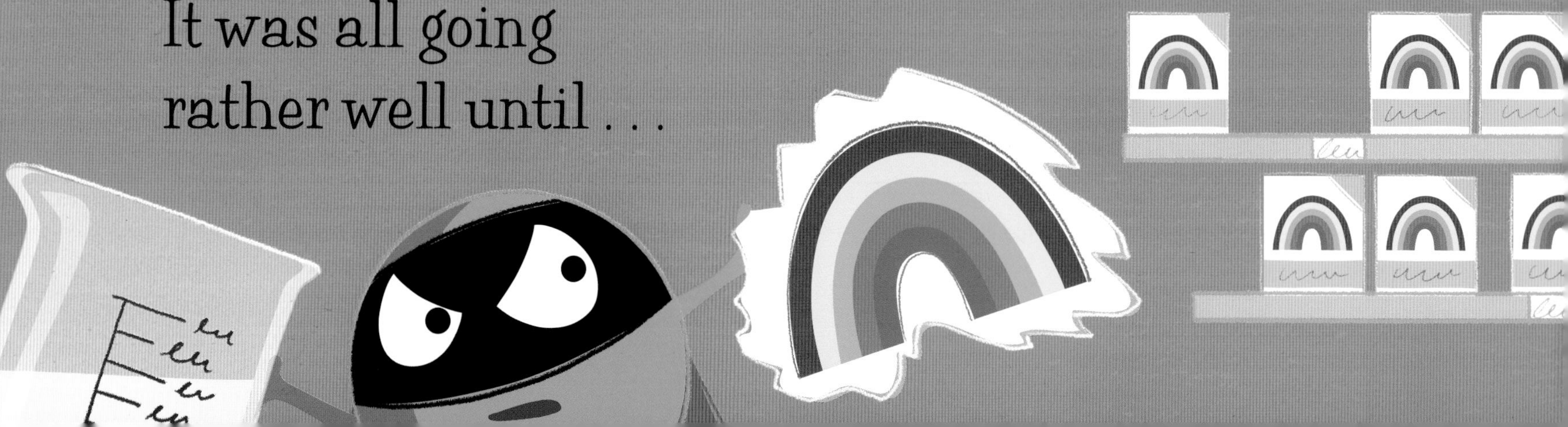

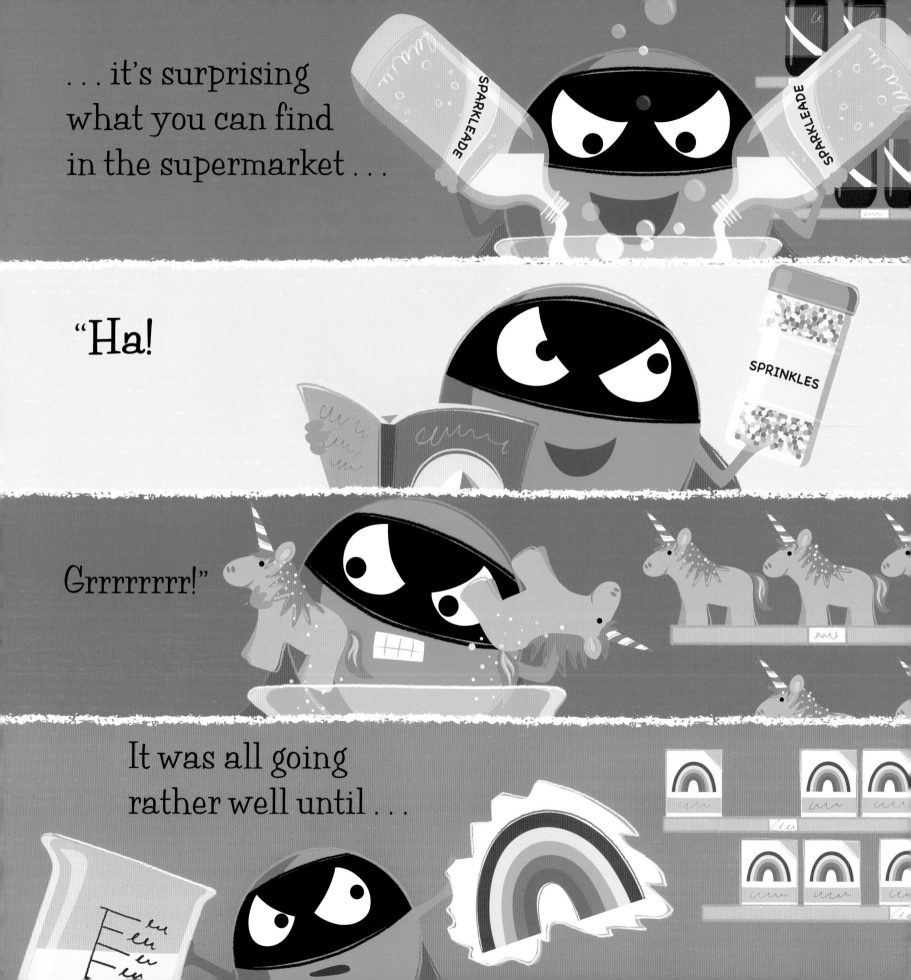

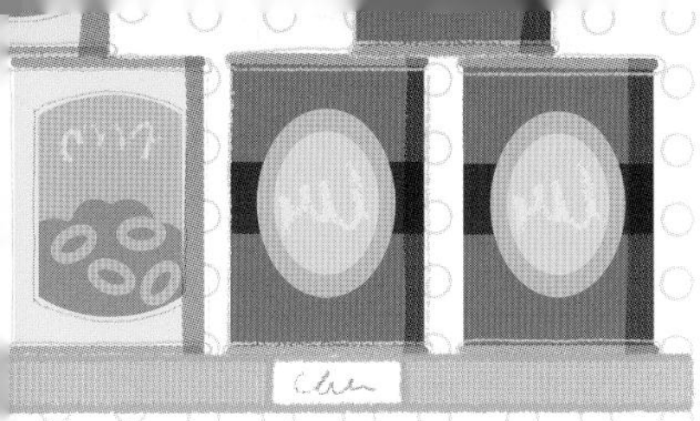

"Where am I going to get
Fluffy Floofiness from?!"
yelled the pea.

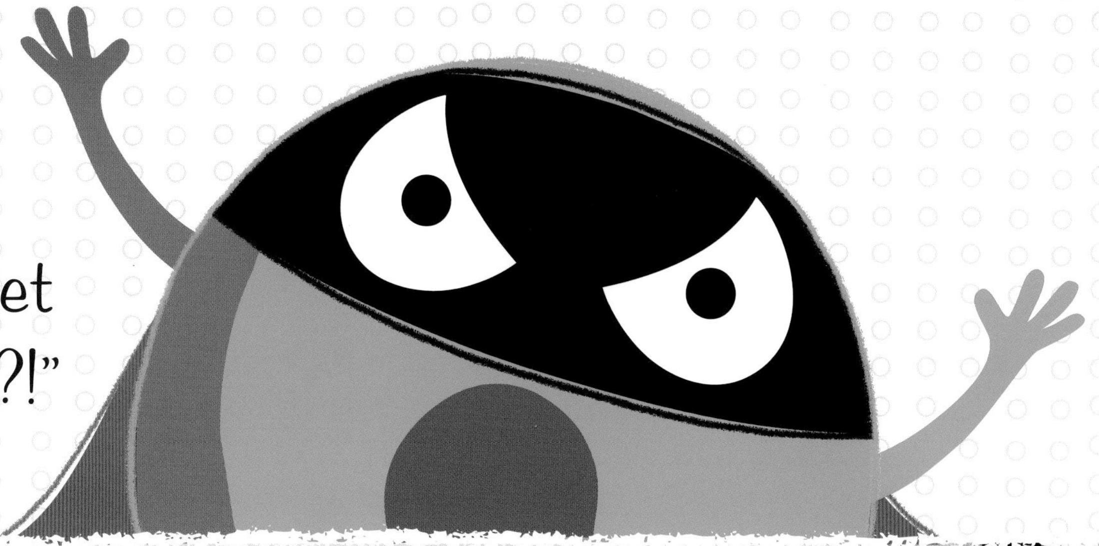

But then it came to him . . .
"Supertato's silly slippers!"

Snip, snip, snip and
in they went.

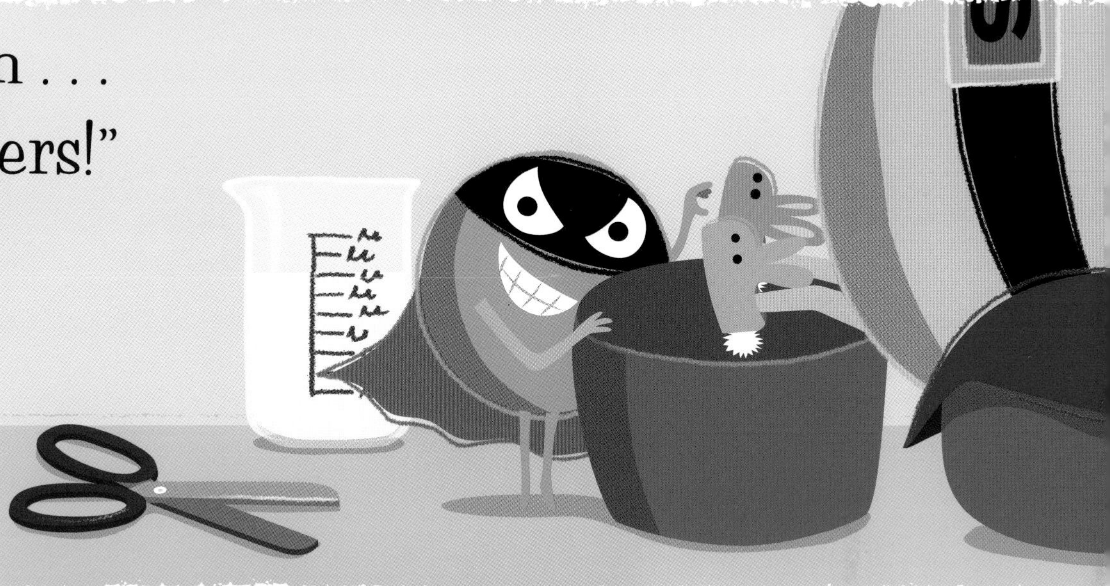

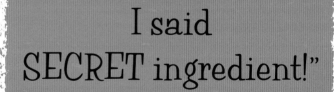

"OK, back to the
recipe. It's time
for the secret
ingredient . . .

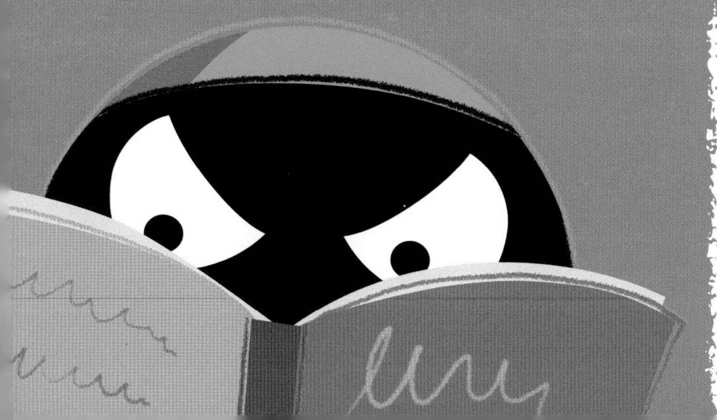

I said
SECRET ingredient!"

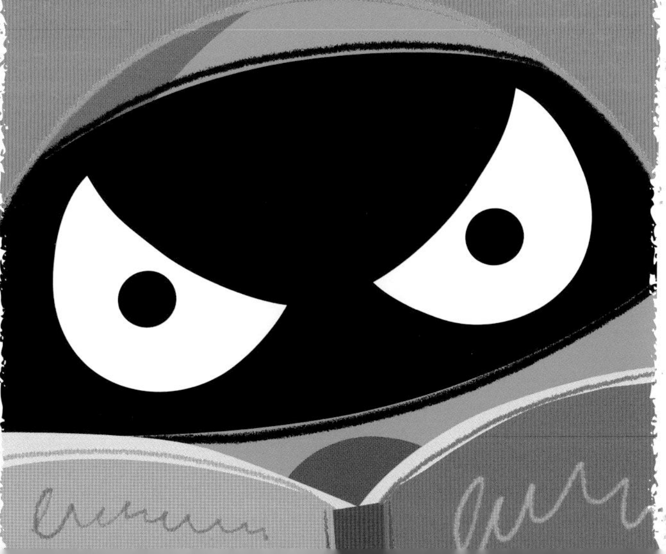

STIR WELL.
FINALLY, POUR INTO
MOULDS AND . . .

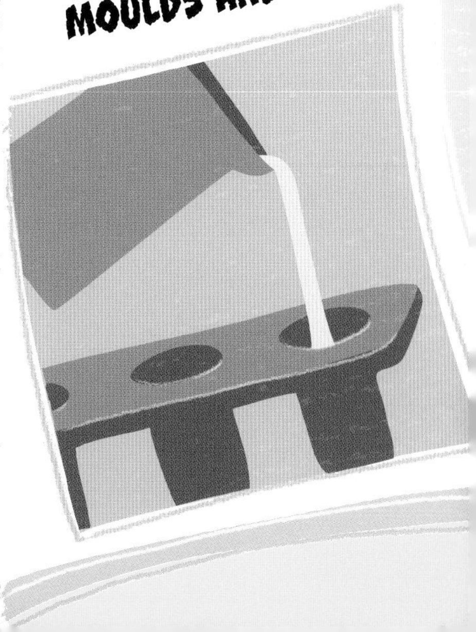

"Ta-da!
Time Crystals!"

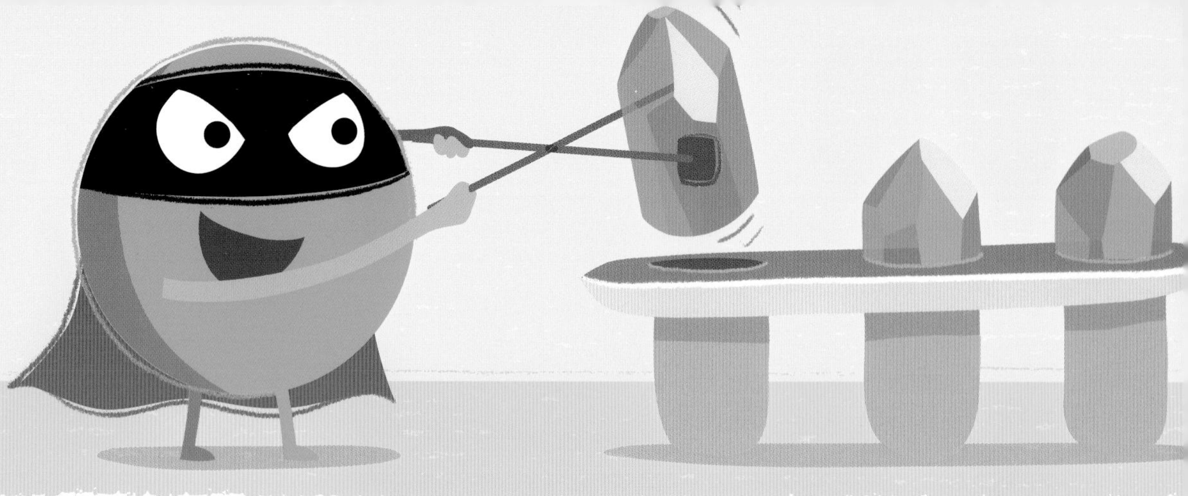

"Oooh, pretty,"
said the little peas.

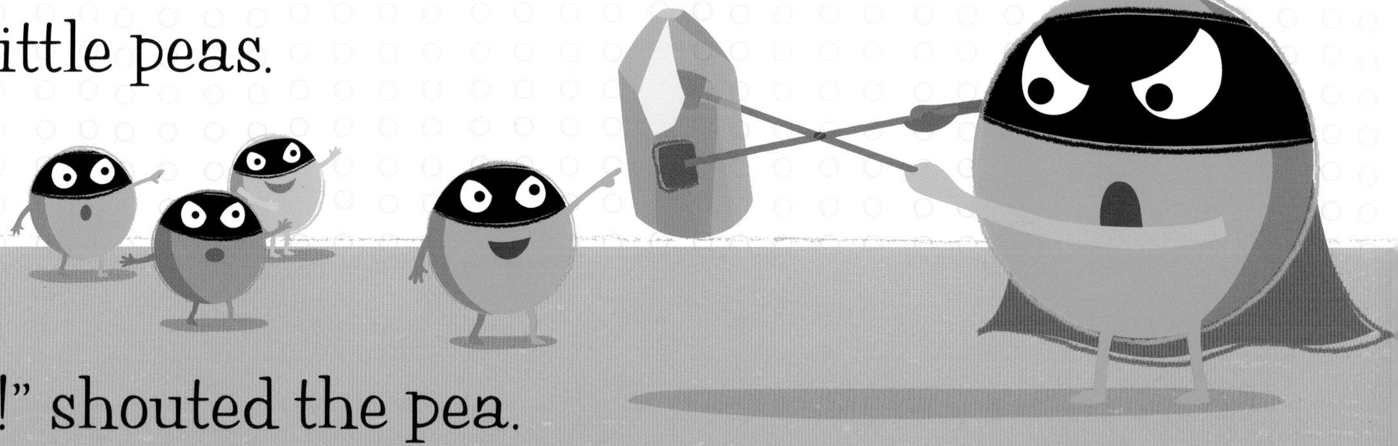

"Get back!" shouted the pea.
"Nobody touches the Time Crystals!
They're far too powerful!

The Time Machine
will need three:
one to get there,
one to get back and
one as a spare.

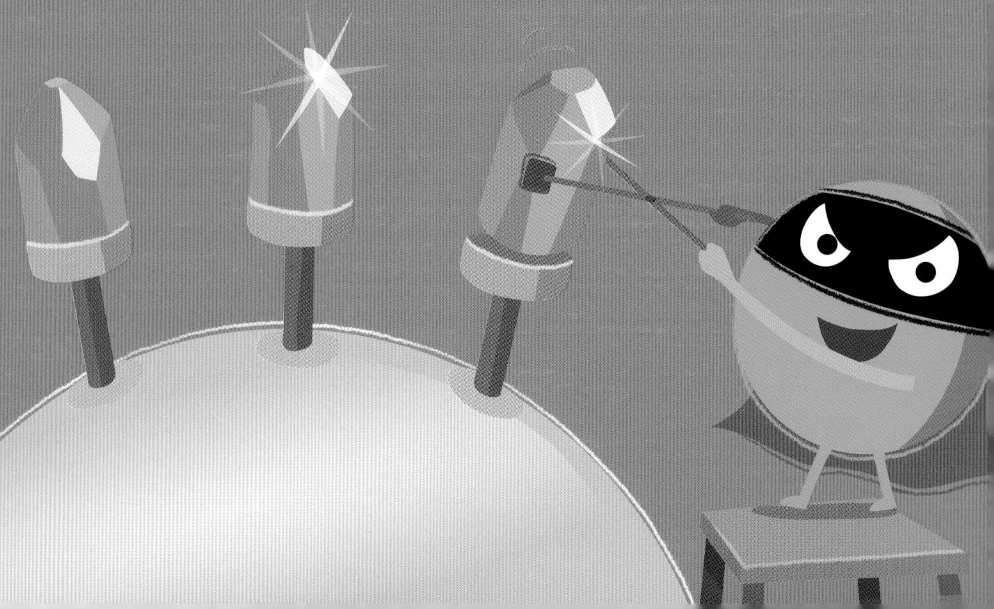

Mwah ha ha ha ha!" cackled the pea.
"Time to go back in time, but first I must set the clock for . . . 'Before Supertato'."

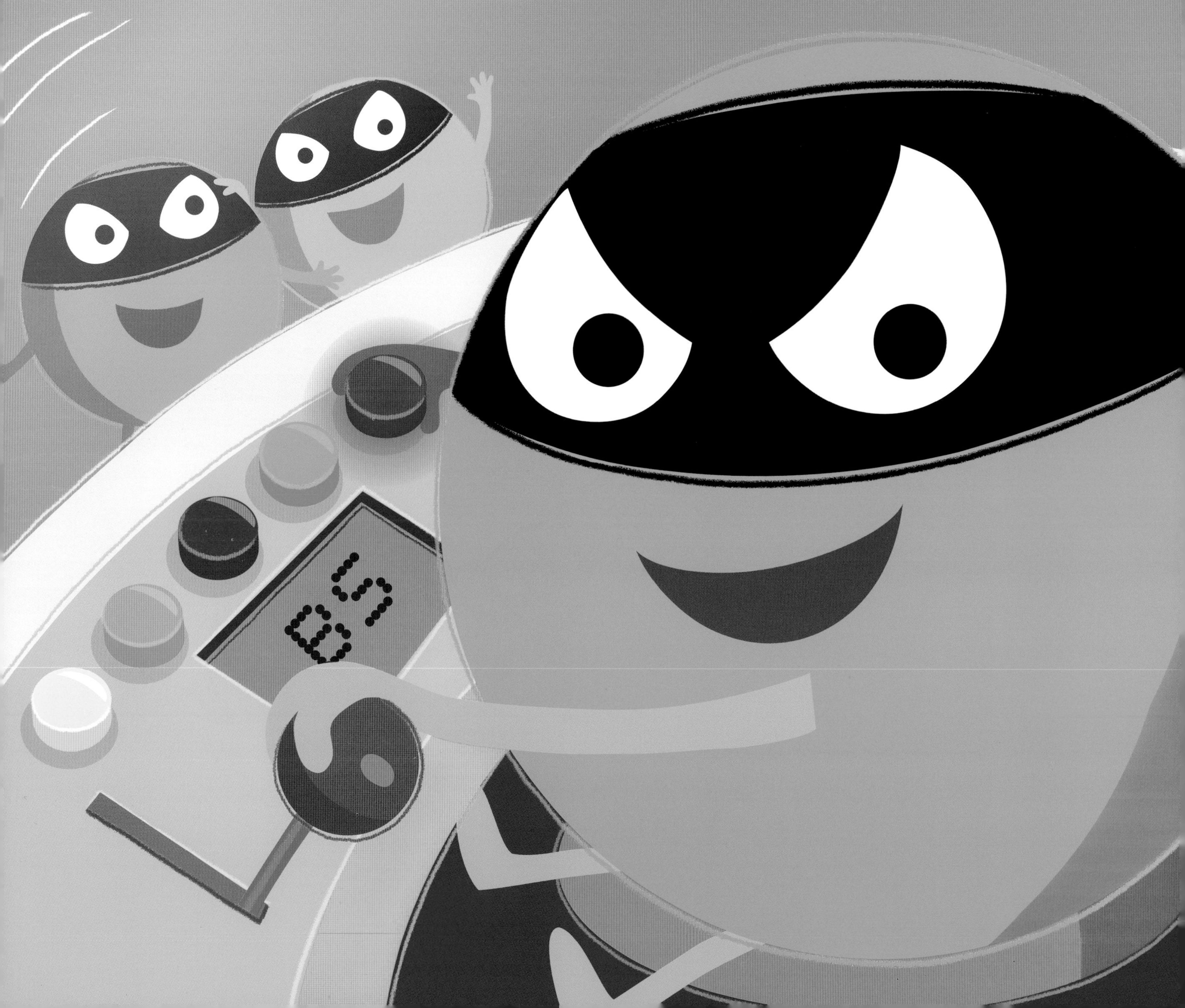

The pea rocketed back through time.

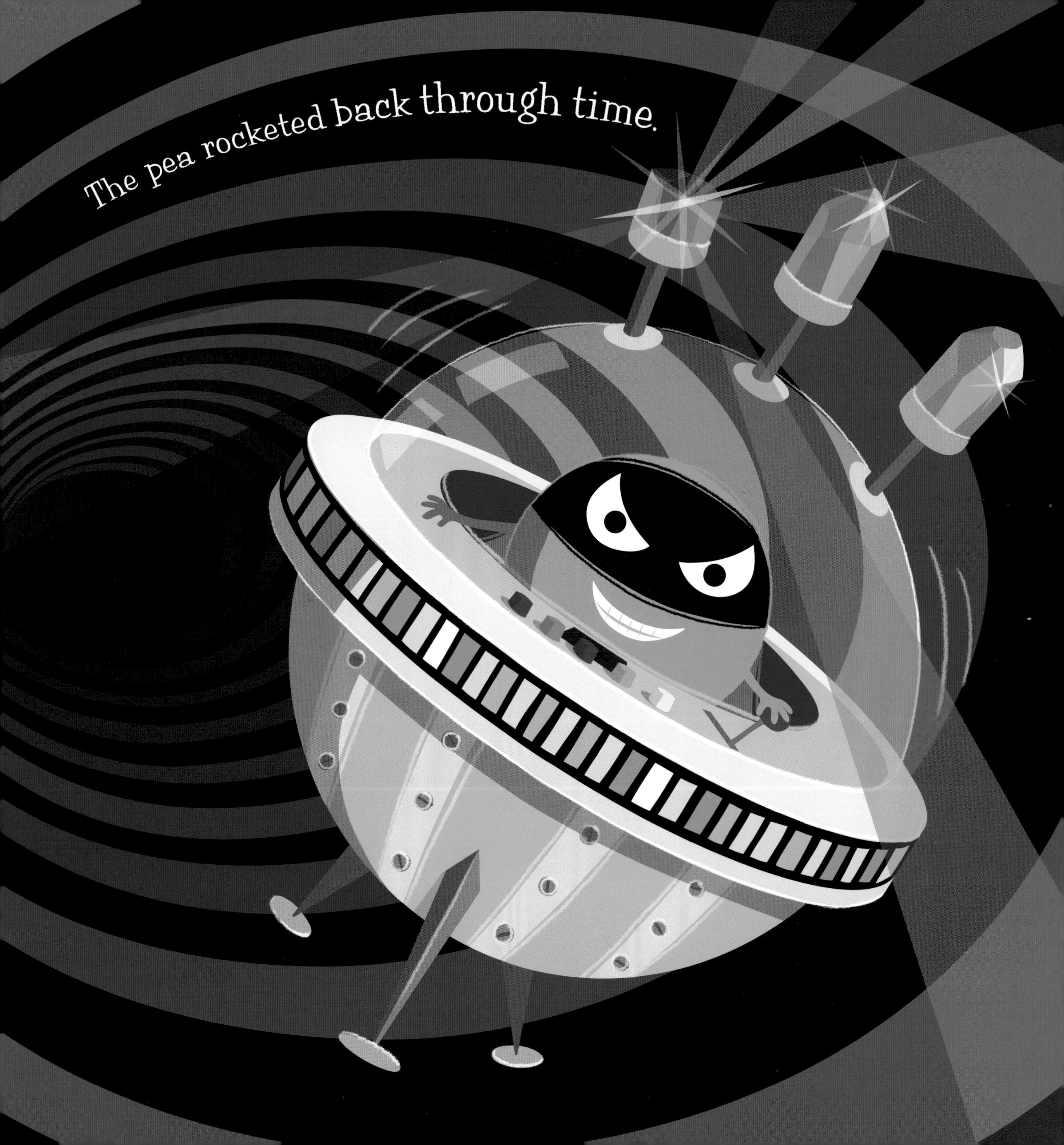

When he finally came to a stop and looked out of the window, he couldn't believe his eyes . . .

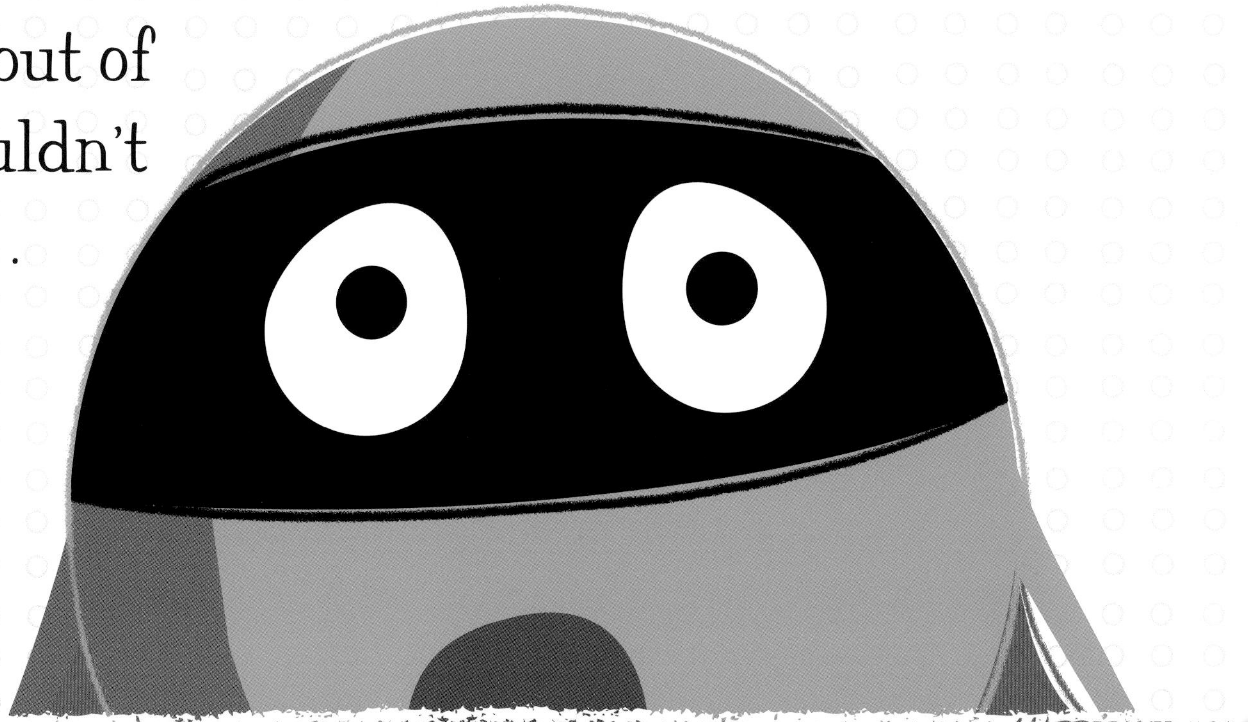

"Dinosaurs! AHHHHHH! Oh, no! I've gone back too far!"

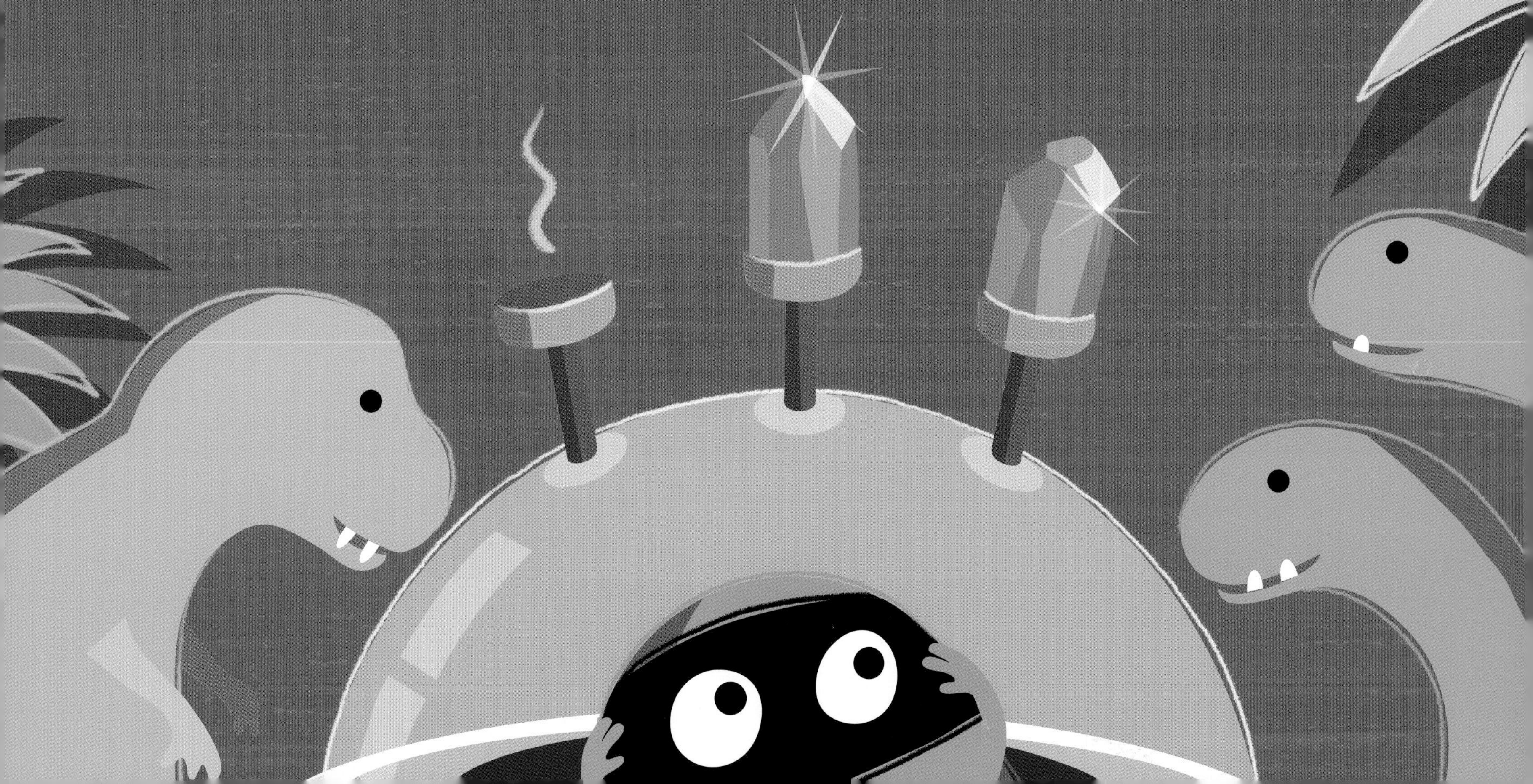

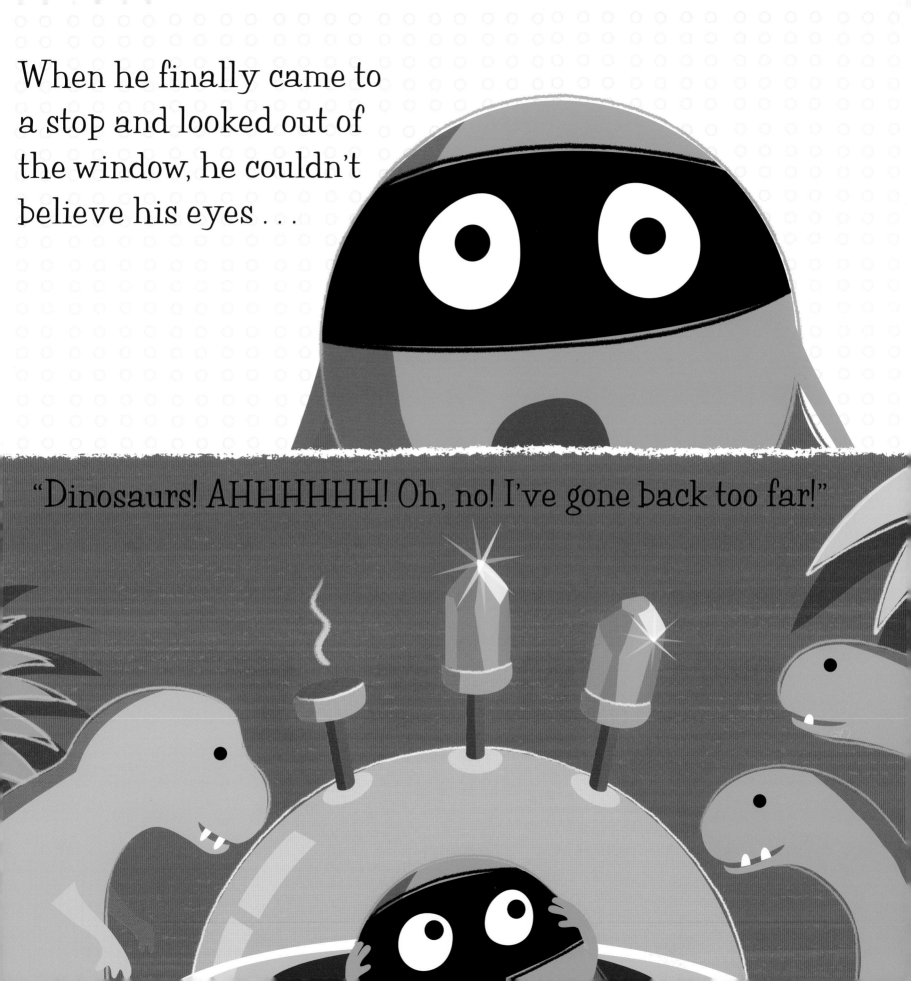

"They're not REAL dinosaurs," giggled Baby Carrot.
"You're just in the toy aisle."

PHEW, thought the pea, looking at the little carrot.
My Time Machine works . . .

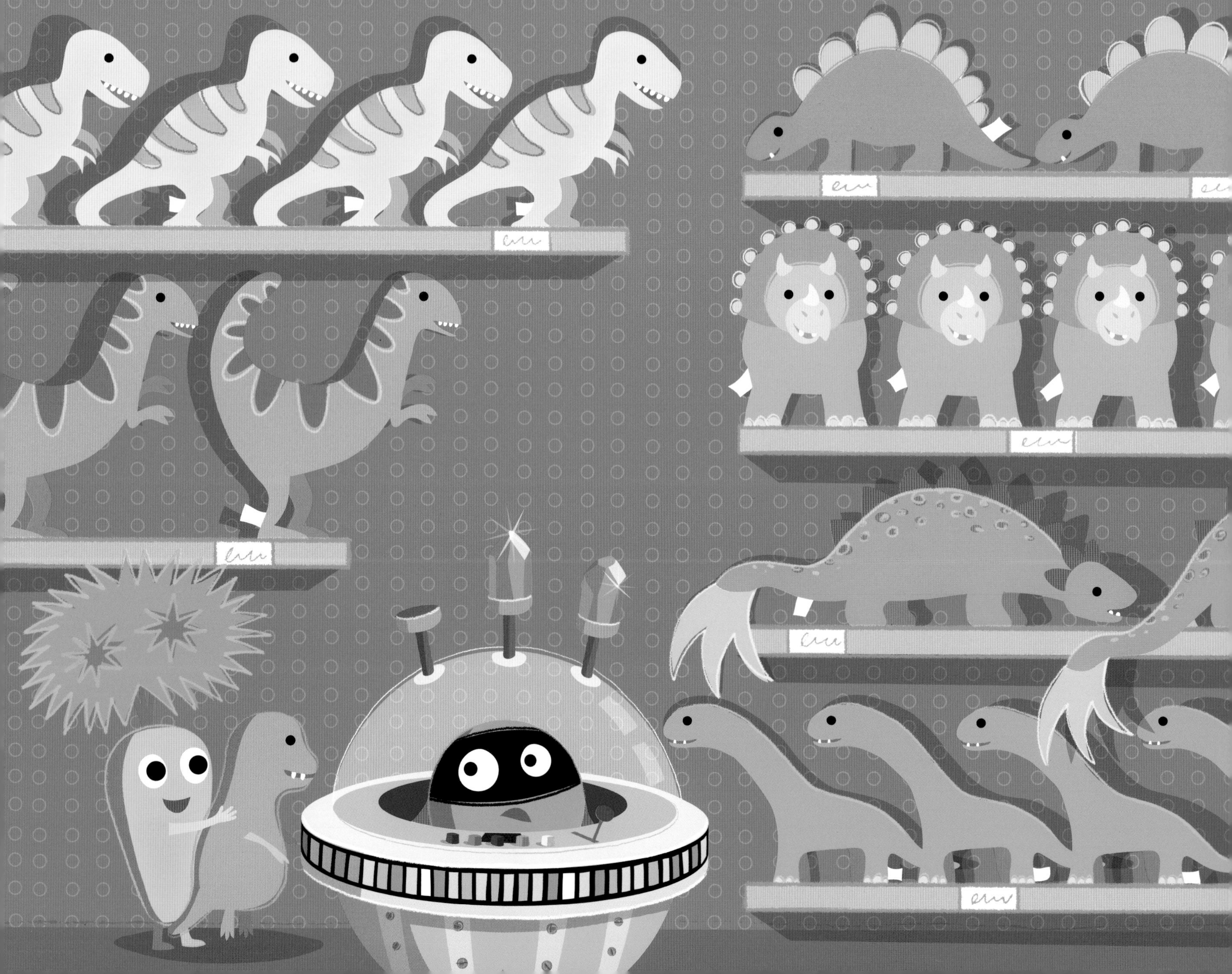

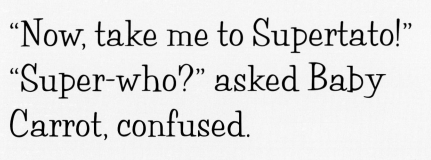

"Now, take me to Supertato!"
"Super-who?" asked Baby
Carrot, confused.

"Do you know a potato?" demanded the pea.
Baby Carrot nodded.
"Then take me to it, you nitwit, and be quick about it!"

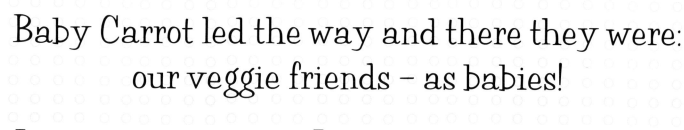

Baby Carrot led the way and there they were:
our veggie friends – as babies!

"Hello, little veggies. Who wants to play a game?"

"Yes, please," said Baby Potato. "What game shall we play?"

"Don't you worry," said The Evil Pea.
"I've got a special game for each one of you . . ."

And with no one to stop him,

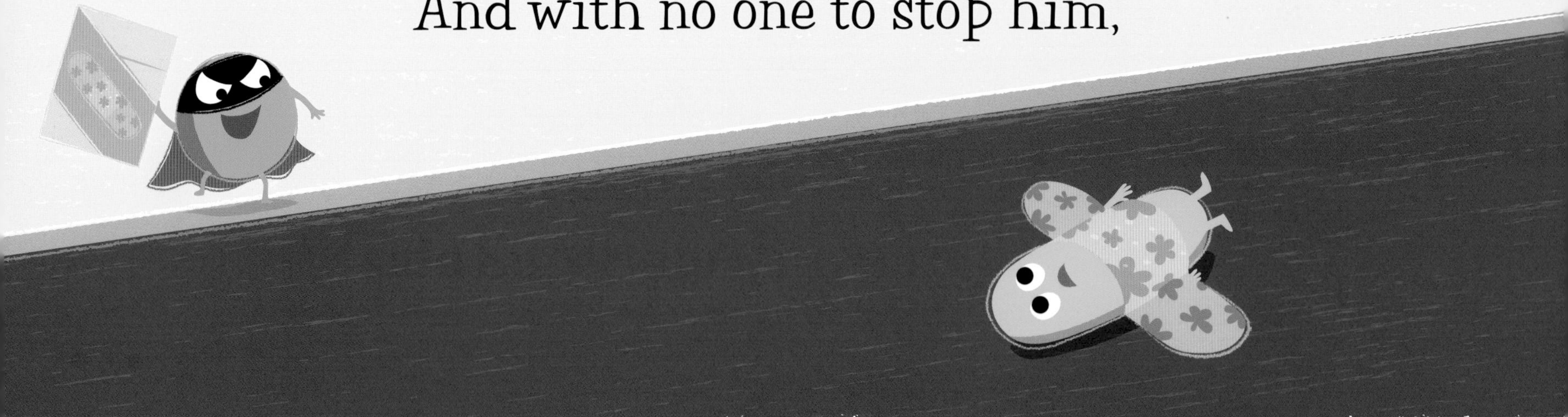

The Evil Pea could do whatever he wanted.

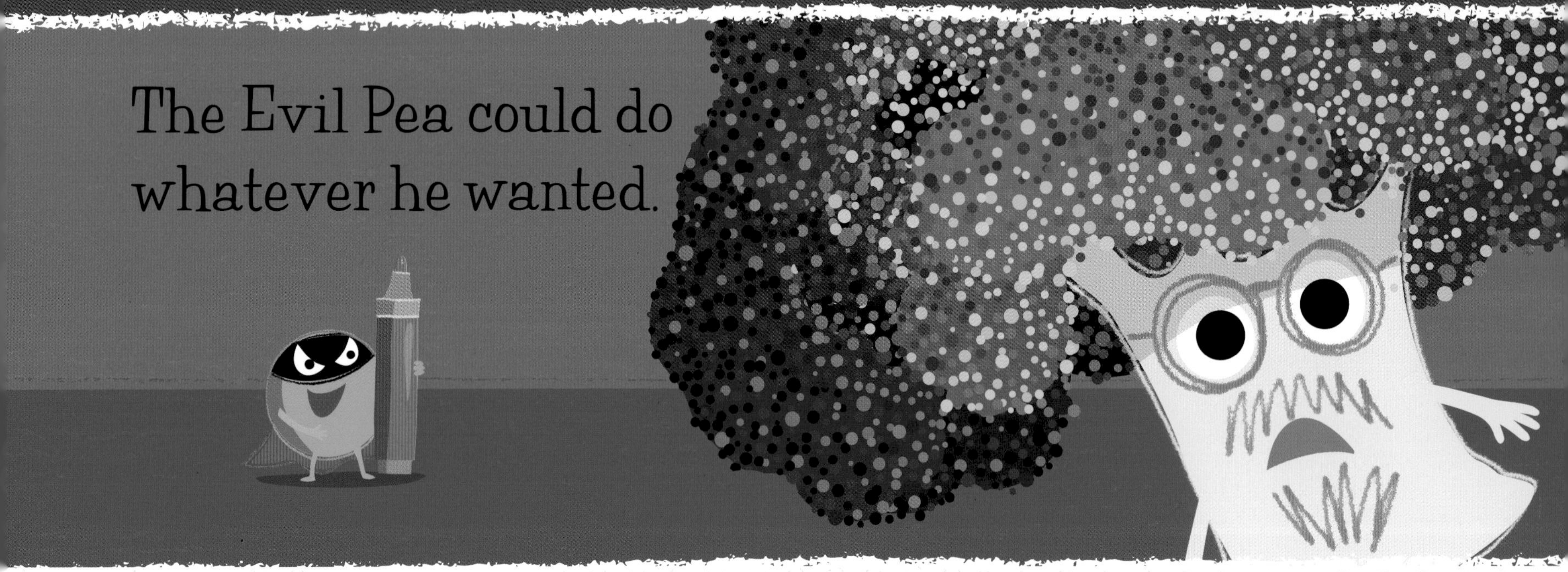

“Is there anyone who can help these baby veggies in distress?

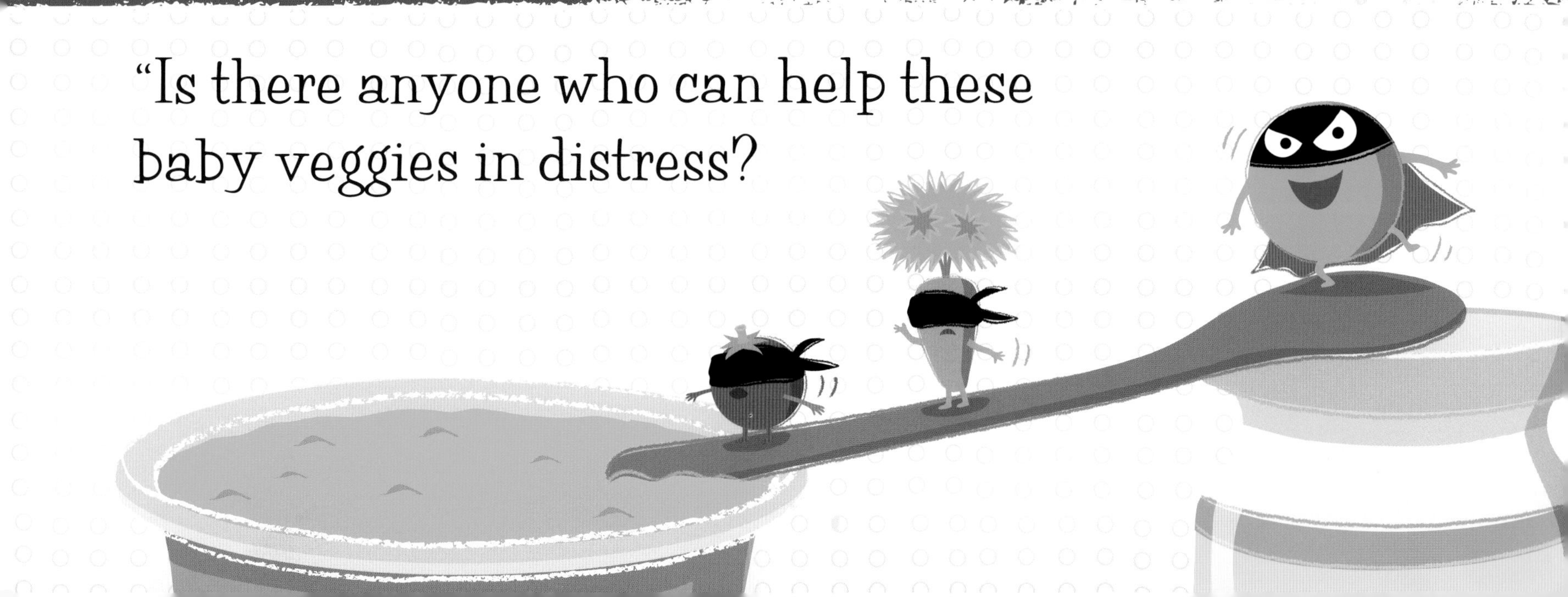

No! Mwah ha ha ha ha!

And now it's time to deal with YOU, poopy-potato."

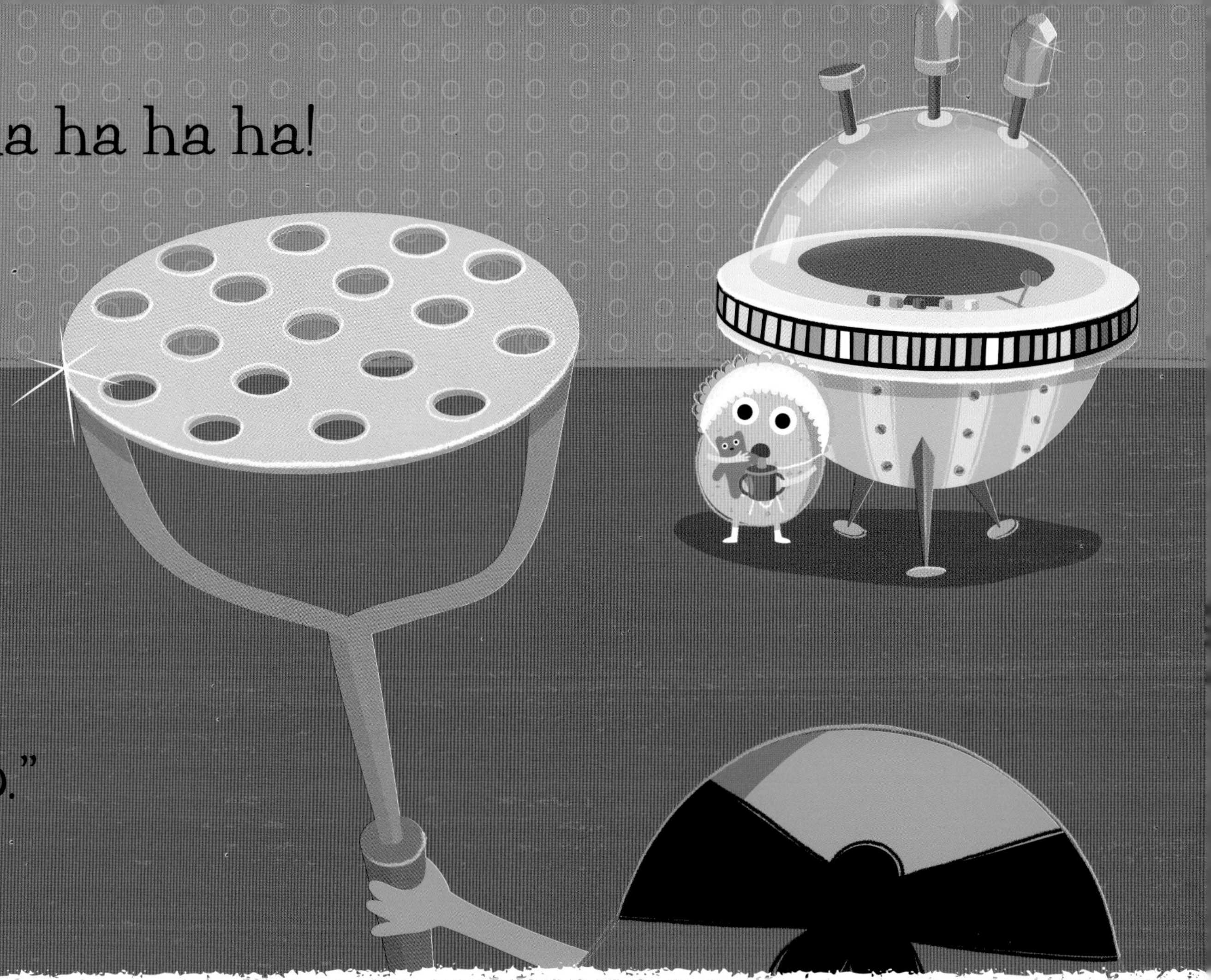

The pea walked towards him menacingly and Baby Potato took a step back . . .

. . . and kept on stepping back and back until . . .

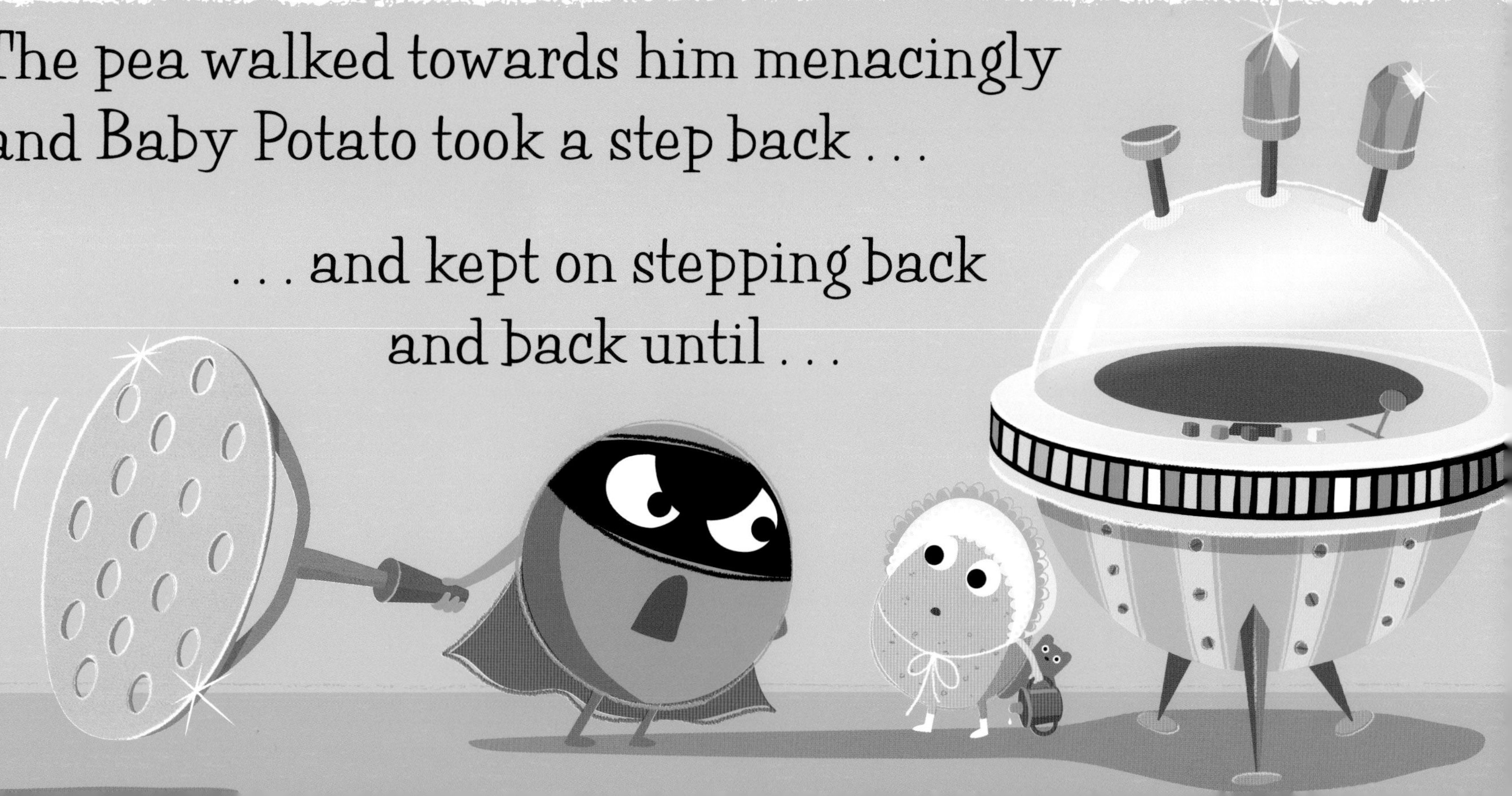

Donk! He bumped into the Time Machine and off flew . . .

. . . one of the Time Crystals!

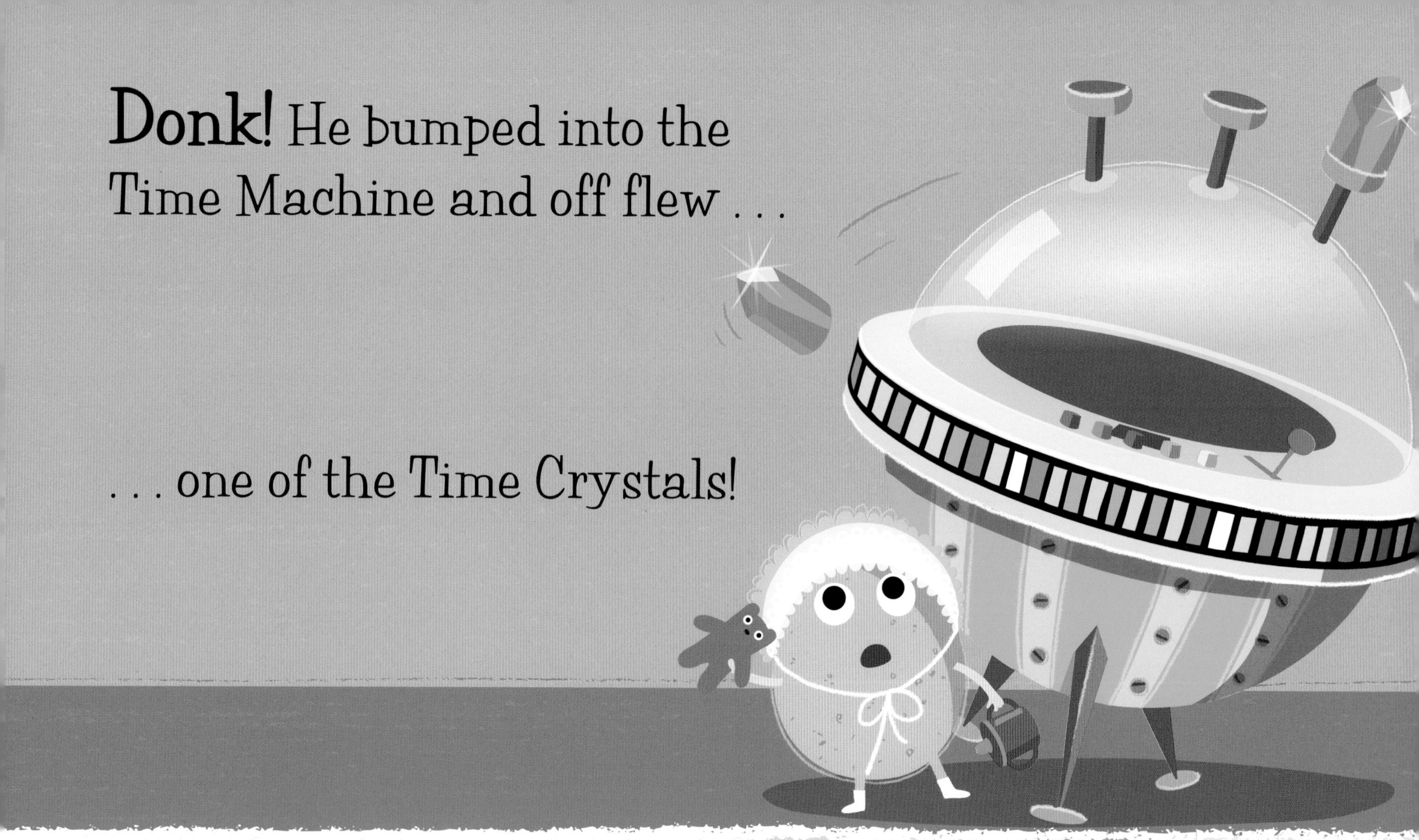

"Oh, excuse me, Mr Pea," he asked, reaching down,

"is this your . . ."

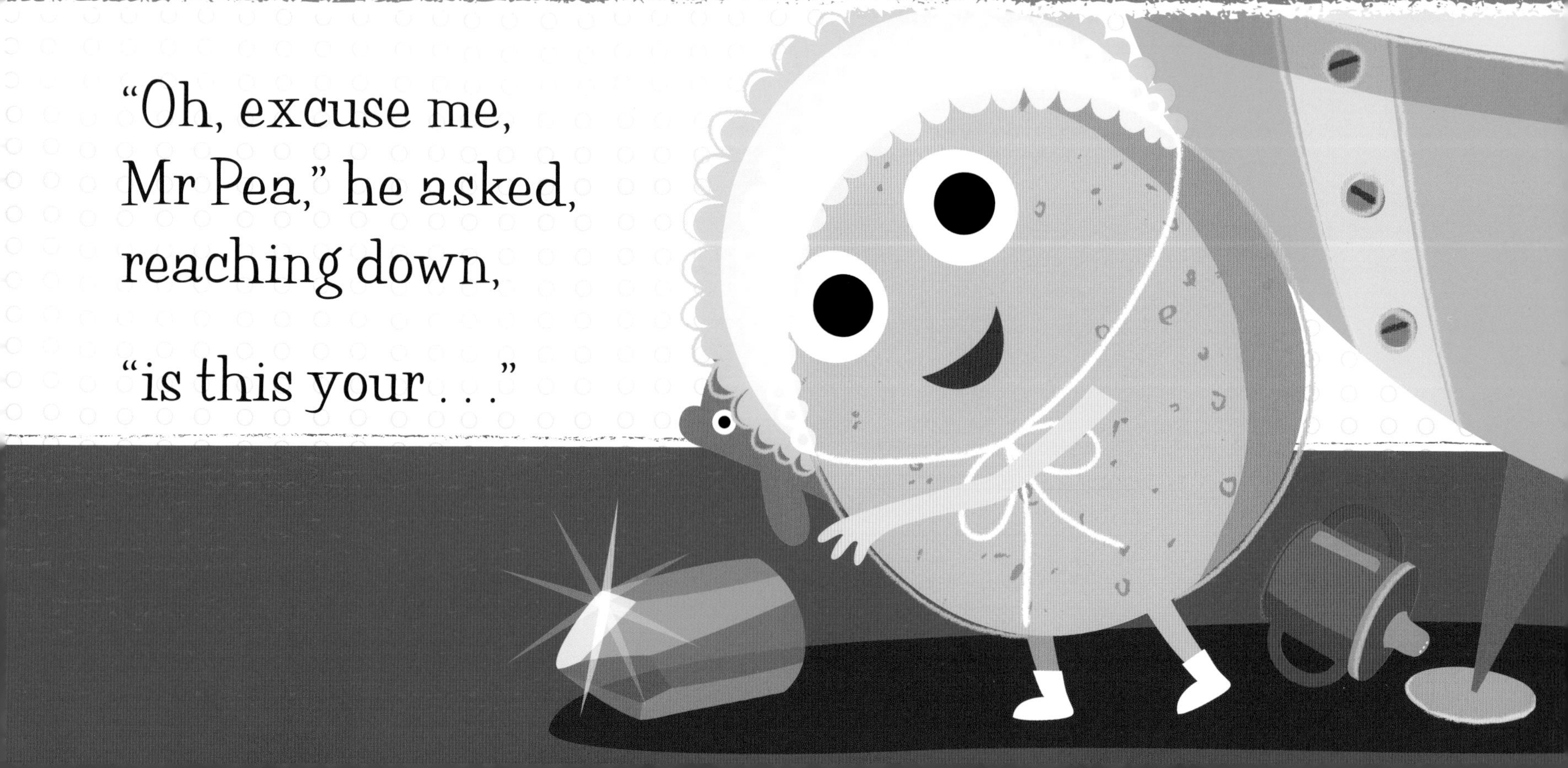

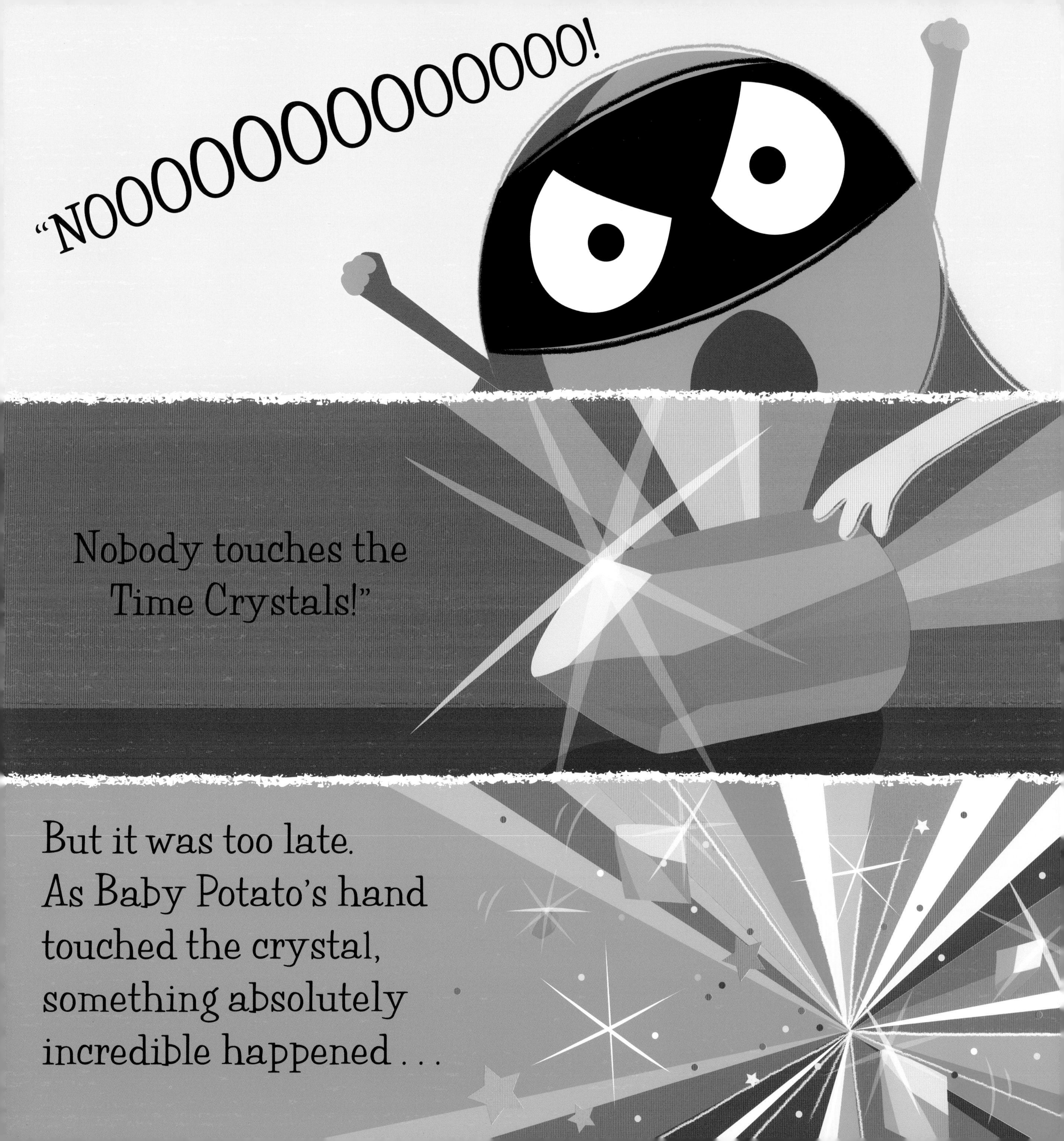

"NOOOOOOOOOOOOO!

Nobody touches the Time Crystals!"

But it was too late. As Baby Potato's hand touched the crystal, something absolutely incredible happened . . .

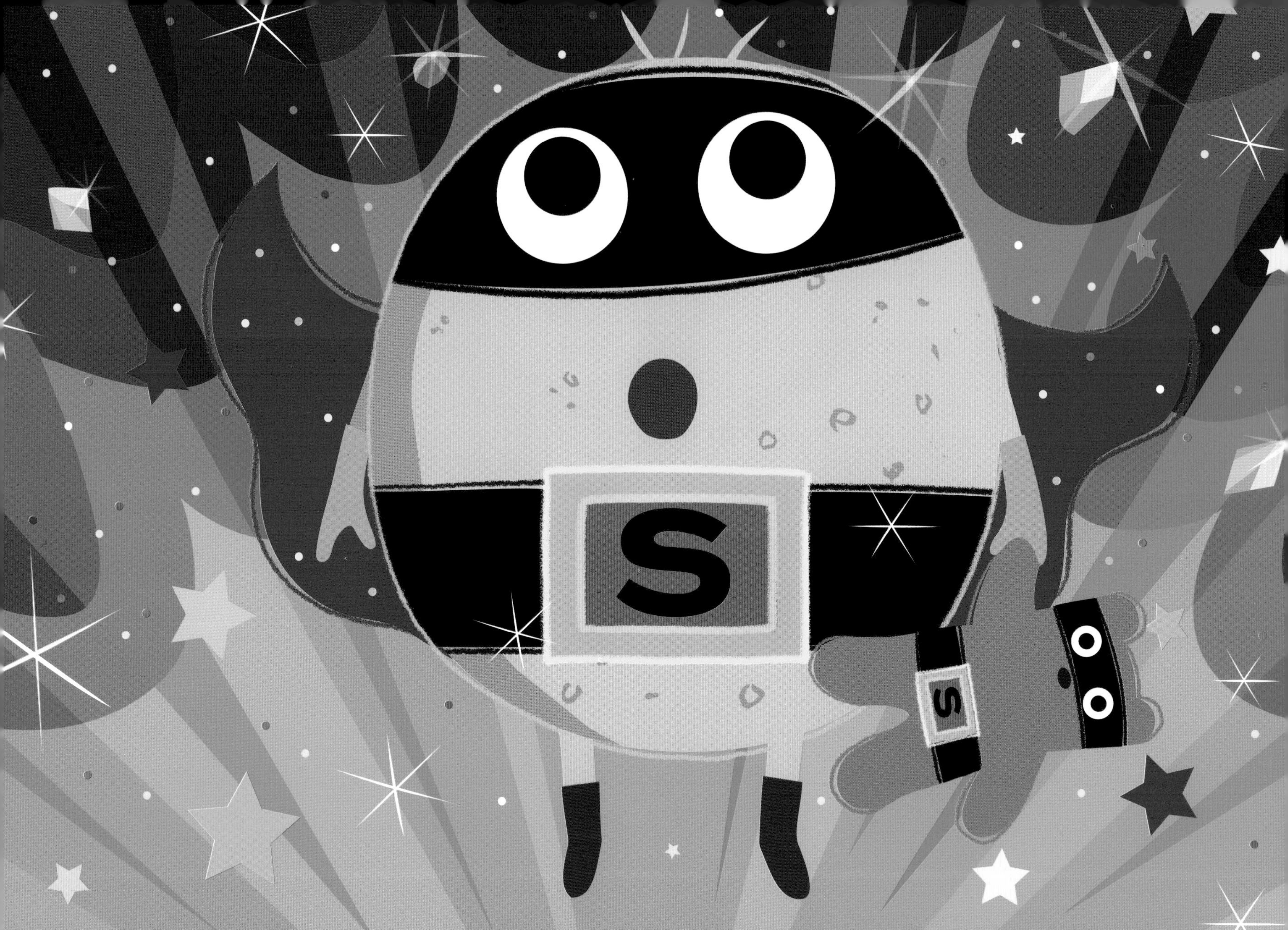

The crystal exploded, sparks flew, rainbows flashed, sprinkles of magical glitter fell from above . . .

SUPERTATO TO THE RESCUE!

"WHA–?"

He used his
newfound strength . . .

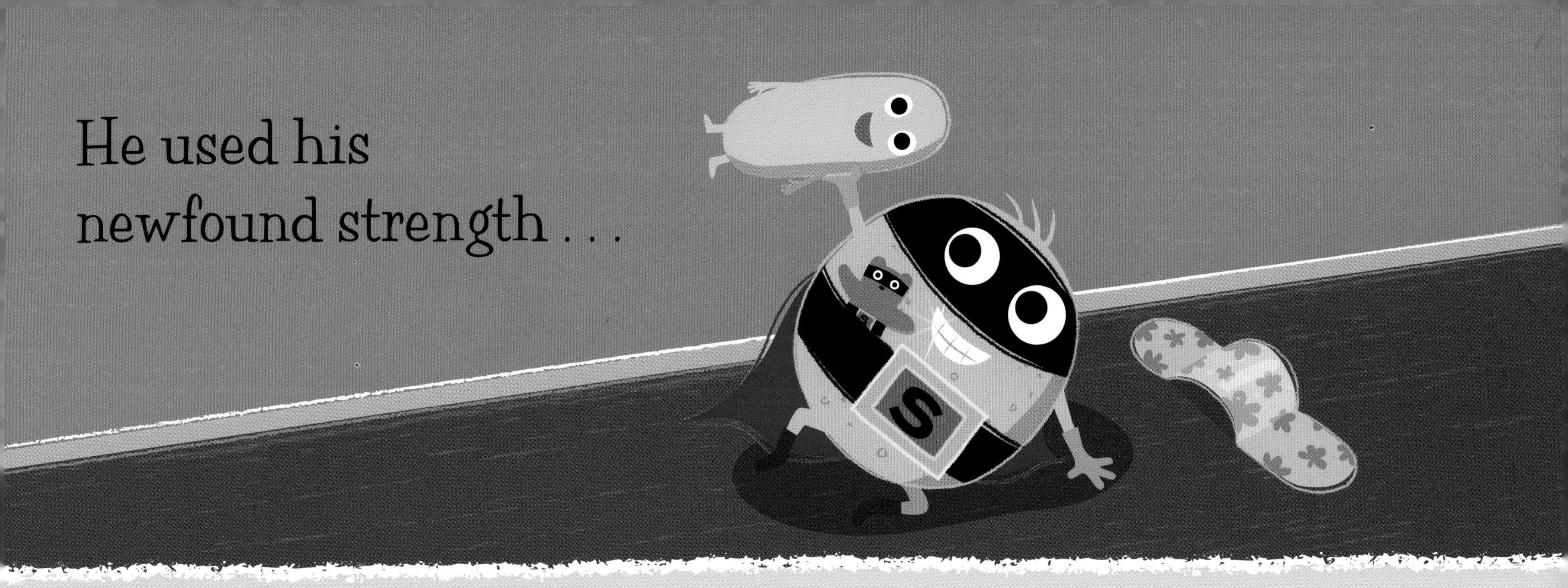

He used his newfound speed . . .

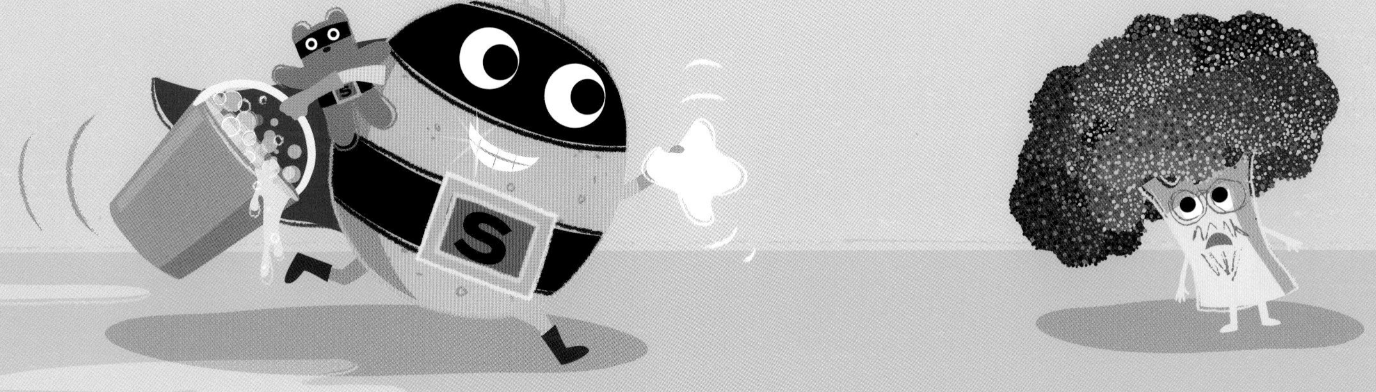

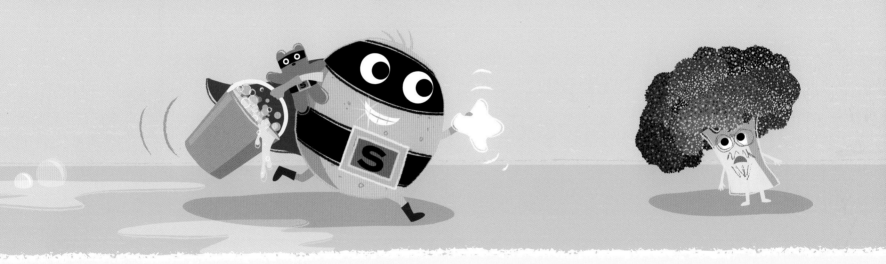

He used his teddy and
a sippy cup . . .

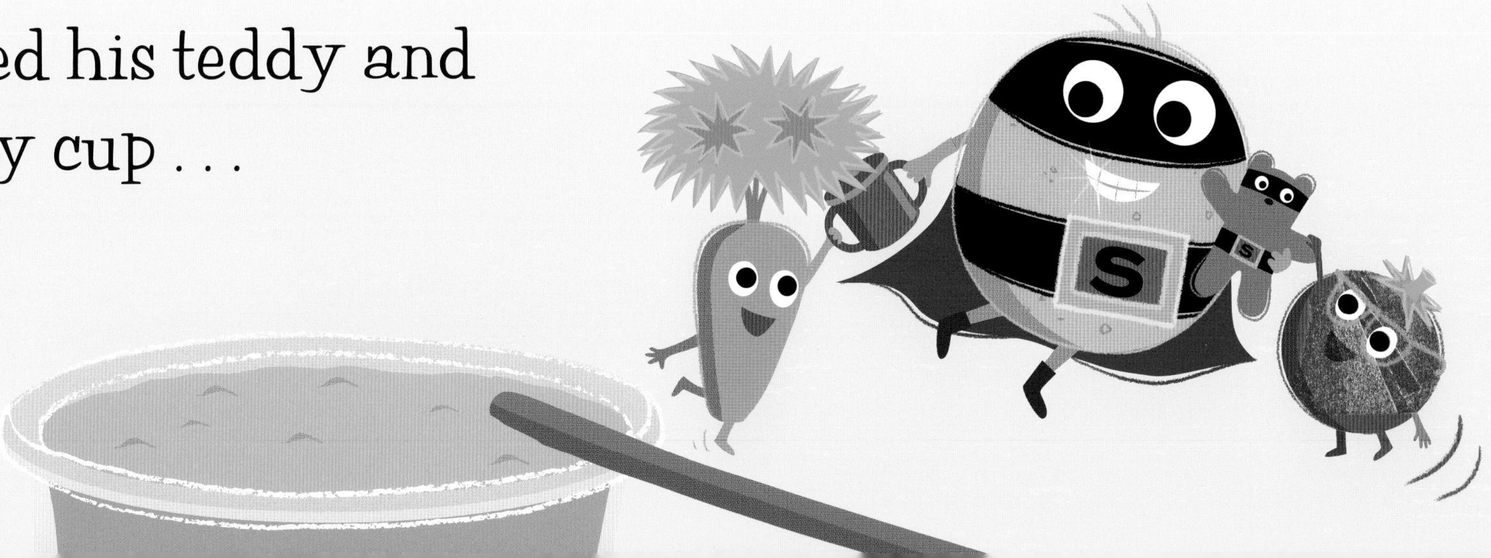

. . . and he saved his baby veggie friends.

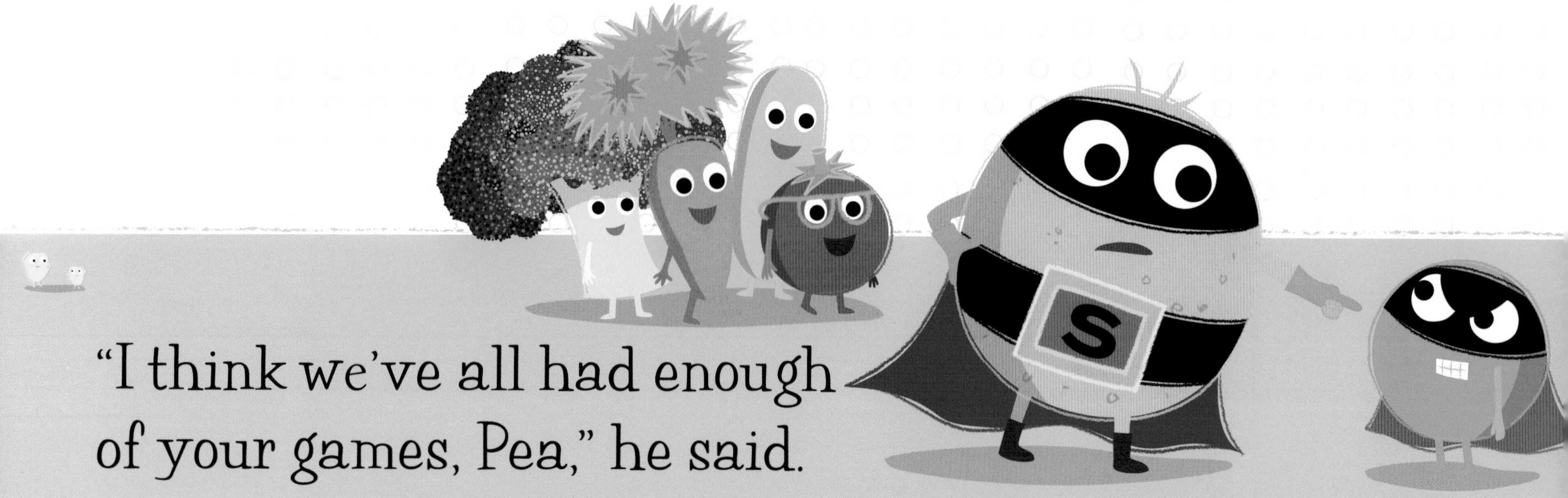

“I think we’ve all had enough of your games, Pea,” he said.

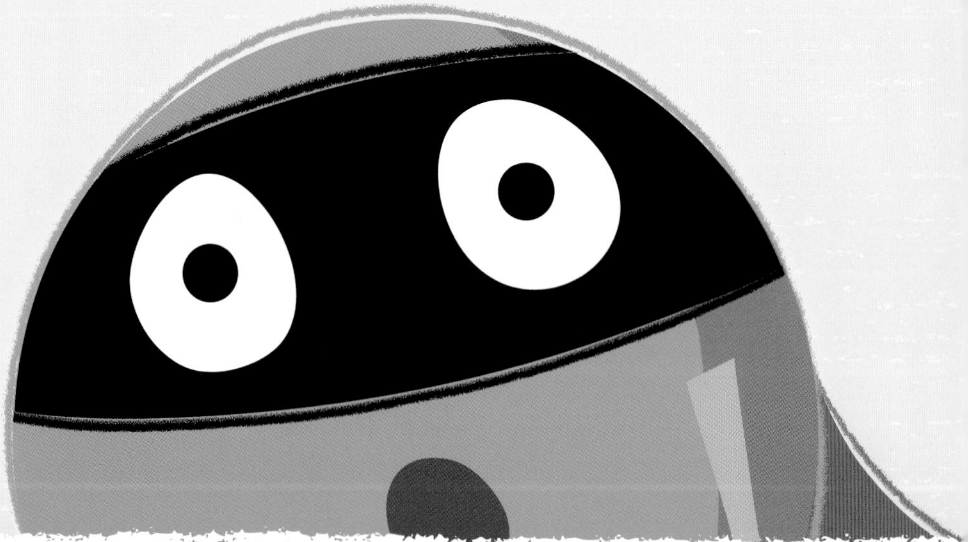

“Uh-oh,” said the pea. “This wasn’t supposed to happen . . .

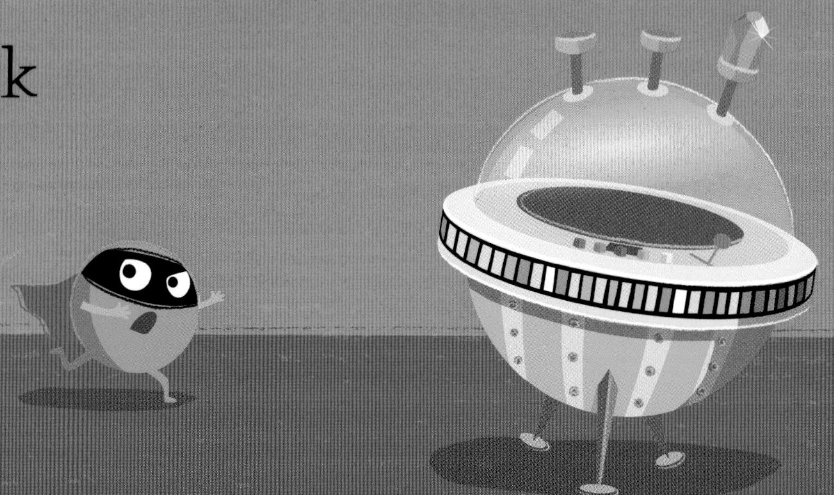

I’m off! I need to get back to the future . . .”

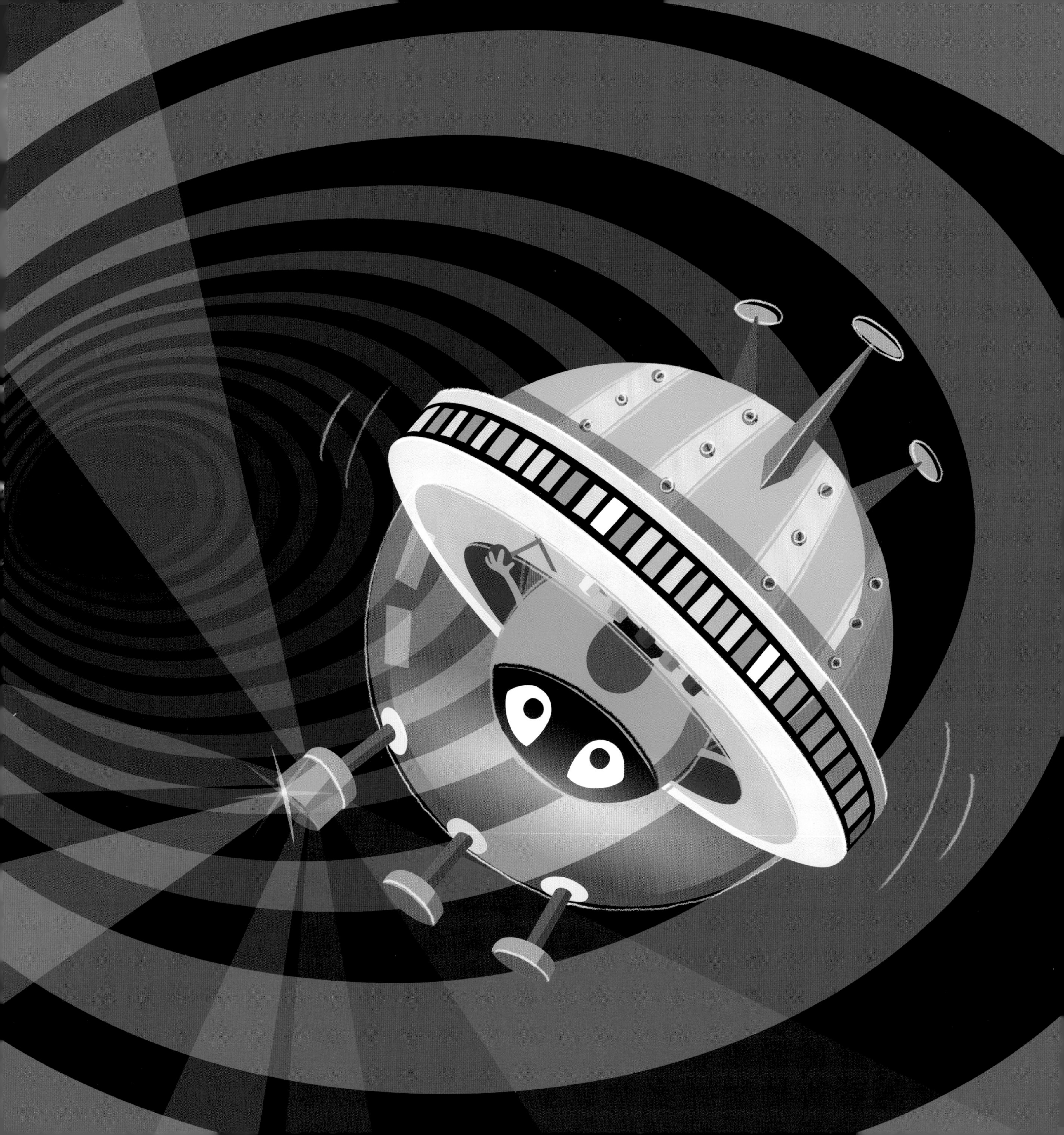

"So you see, veggies, it's actually all thanks to the pea that I have my superpowers. Pea, I don't think I can ever thank you enough," said Supertato with a smile.

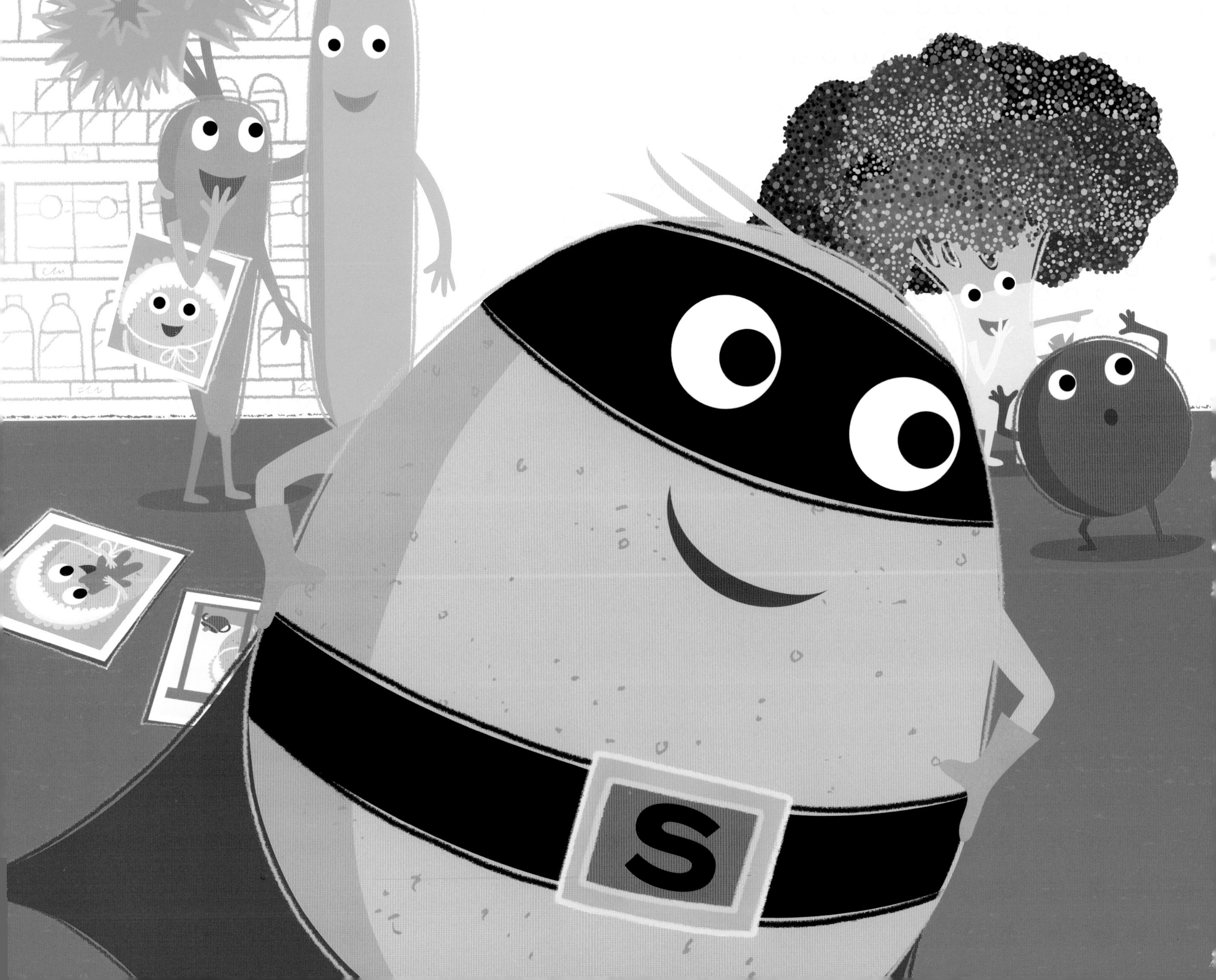
S

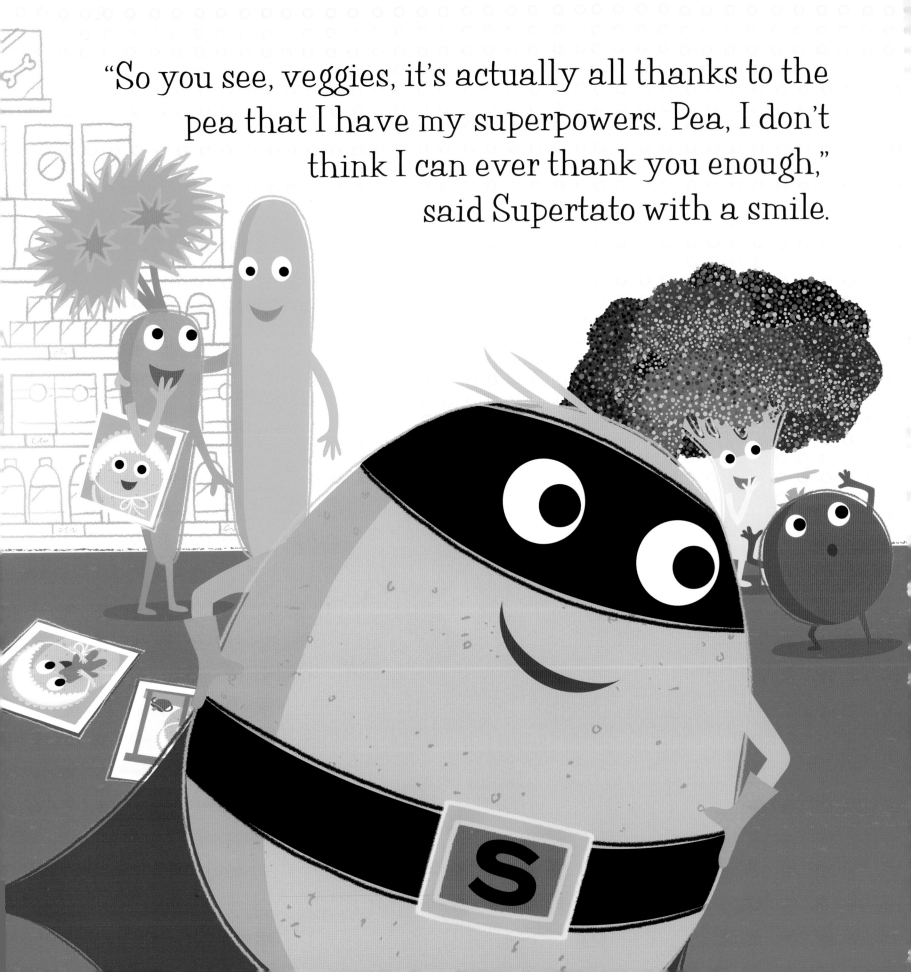

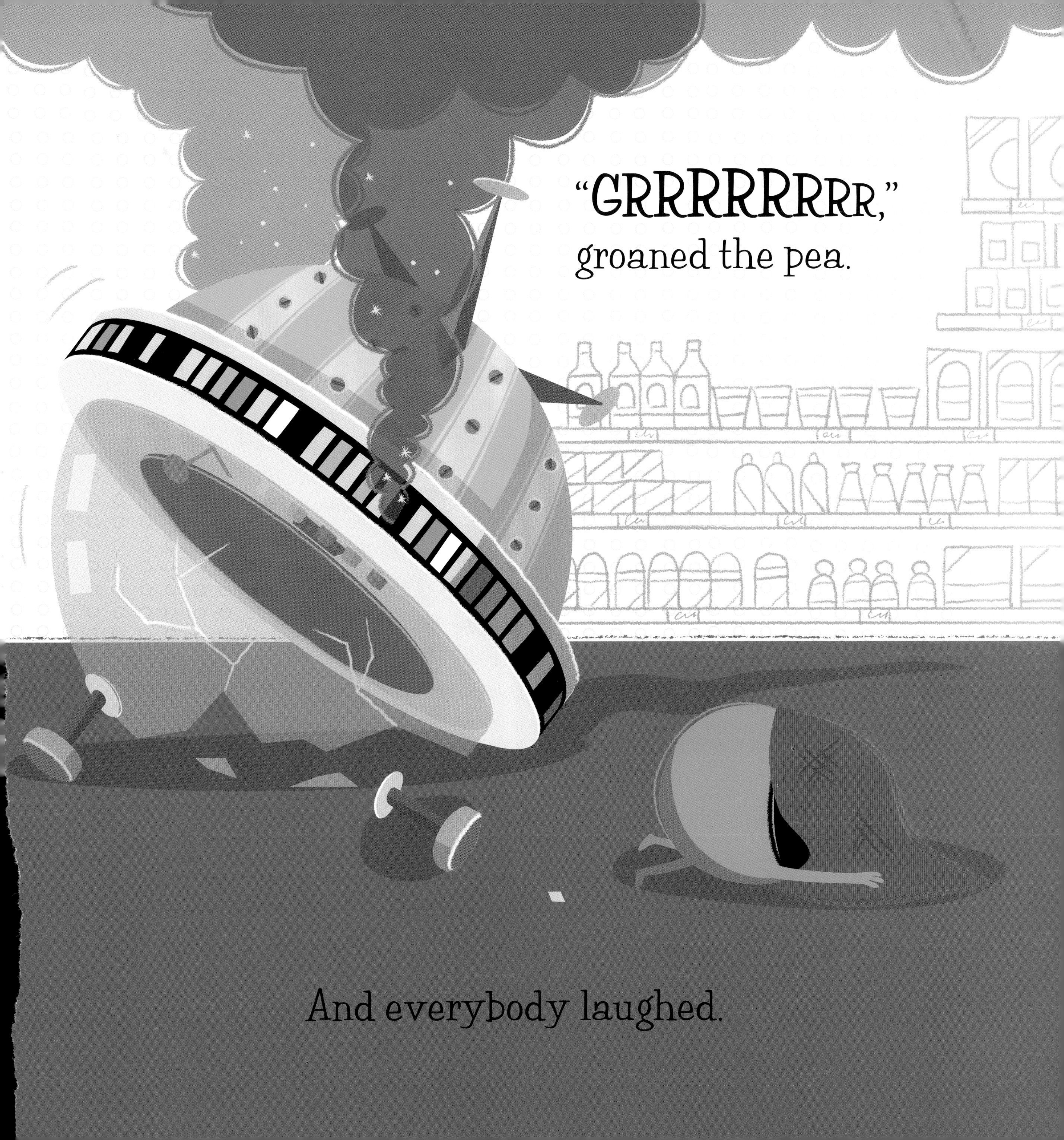

"GRRRRRRRR," groaned the pea.

And everybody laughed.

SUE HENDRA & PAUL LINNET
SUPERTATO

SUE HENDRA
PAUL LINNET
SUPERTATO
VEGGIES ASSEMBLE

SUE HENDRA
PAUL LINNET
SUPERTATO
RUN, VEGGIES, RUN!

SUPERTATO
EVIL PEA RULES!
SUE HENDRA & PAUL LINNET

SUPERTATO
VEGGIES IN THE VALLEY OF DOOM
SUE HENDRA
PAUL LINNET

SUPERTATO
CARNIVAL CATASTRO-PEA!

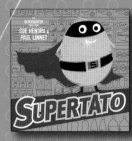

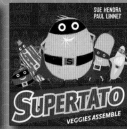

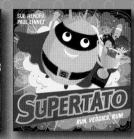

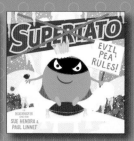

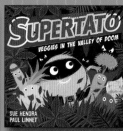

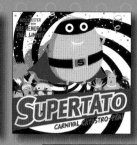

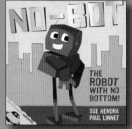

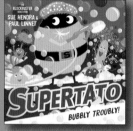

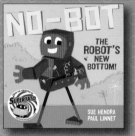

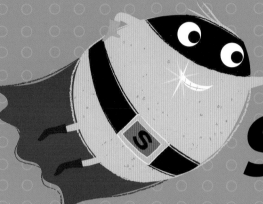

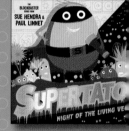

If you like

SUPERTATO

MEAN GREEN TIME MACHINE

you'll love these other adventures from

SUE HENDRA & PAUL LINNET

NO-BOT
THE ROBOT WITH NO BOTTOM!
SUE HENDRA
PAUL LINNET

NO-BOT
THE ROBOT'S NEW BOTTOM!
SUE HENDRA
PAUL LINNET

BARRY
THE FISH WITH FINGERS
SUE HENDRA
PAUL LINNET

BARRY
THE FISH WITH FINGERS AND THE HAIRY SCARY MONSTER
SUE HENDRA
PAUL LINNET

SUE HENDRA
PAUL LINNET
I NEED A WEE!

SUE HENDRA & PAUL LINNET
SUPERTATO
BUBBLY TROUBLY!

SUE HENDRA & PAUL LINNET
SUPERTATO
NIGHT OF THE LIVING VE

THE BLOCKBUSTER SERIES FROM
SUE HENDRA & PAUL LINNET
SUPERTATO
THE GREAT EGGSCAPE!

SUPERTATO
EVIL PEA
JACK AND THE BEANSTALK
THE BLOCKBUSTER SERIES FROM
SUE HENDRA & PAUL LINNET

I SPY ISLAND
SUE HENDRA & PAUL LINNET

SUE HENDRA
PAUL LINNET

GORDON'S GREAT ESCAPE
SUE HENDRA
PAUL LINNET

KEITH
THE CAT WITH THE MAGIC HAT

NORMAN
THE SLUG WITH THE SILLY SHELL
SUE HENDRA
PAUL LINNET

NORMAN
THE SLUG WHO SAVED CHRISTMAS
SUE HENDRA
PAUL LINNET

I SPY ISLAND
BOOK VS. SHARK
SUE HENDRA
PAUL LINNET

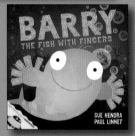

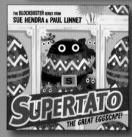

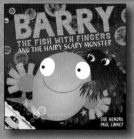

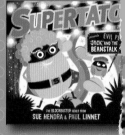

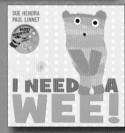

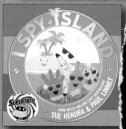

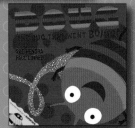

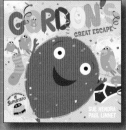

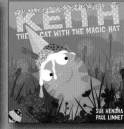

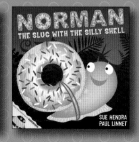

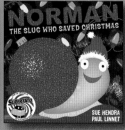

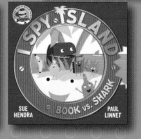